Also by Barbara Brooks Wallace

Peppermints in the Parlor

The Barrel
IN THE *Basement*

BARBARA BROOKS WALLACE

The Barrel

IN THE

Basement

Illustrated by Sharon Wooding

ATHENEUM 1985 NEW YORK

Library of Congress Cataloging in Publication Data

Wallace, Barbara Brooks
The barrel in the basement.

SUMMARY: Pudding, the youngest of three
elves, living in a barrel in the basement of a human
named Noah, proves that he is capable of
great deeds like the heroes of the past.
1. Children's stories, American. H. Fairies—
Fiction] I. Wooding, Sharon, ill. II. Title.
PZ7.W1547Bar   1985   [Fic]   84-21521
ISBN 0-689-31105-2

Text copyright © 1985 by Barbara Brooks Wallace
Pictures copyright © 1985 by Atheneum Publishers, Inc.
All rights reserved
Published simultaneously in Canada by
McClelland & Stewart, Ltd.
Composition by Heritage Press, Charlotte,
North Carolina
Printed and bound by Fairfield Graphics, Inc.,
Fairfield, Pennsylvania
Designed by Mary Ahern
First Edition

THIS BOOK IS FOR
Betty Brock,
Larry Callen
and Jean Karl

Contents

PROLOGUE

The sheet billowed out over the bed like the wind-filled sails of an old sea vessel, then was suddenly whipped back and snapped down on the bed by the determined gray-headed housekeeper.

"There now, you'd better hurry with the windows," she said to a young girl of sixteen or seventeen years, who was to all intents and purposes dusting off the windowsill, but was spending more time dreamily watching stormy raindrops blowing across the windowpane.

The housekeeper sighed wearily, then gave the sheet a sharp pull over the edges and began to form a tight, neat corner. "There's the floor to be scrubbed still, and we can't take all day. There'll be another one for this bed before the afternoon is out. They come and they go." She sighed again. "One goes out, and the other comes in."

The girl looked questioningly at the old housekeeper. "Being new here and all, m'um, I don't know much about it, but is it true what they say? I mean about the one in this room just . . . disappearing into thin air, as it were."

The housekeeper folded another corner and stood back to examine it critically. "A real nice old gentleman," she muttered, ignoring the question.

The girl glanced at the housekeeper sideways. "It was strange he didn't leave a note or anything. Is it true what they say, that there was . . . foul play?"

"Oh, they always say that. Foul play is always suspected when someone just . . . vanishes. But there's much too much saying going on in this place if you ask me!" The housekeeper gave a disapproving sniff. "If I were you, I'd just go on about my business and not encourage any of it." Her mouth clamped shut as if this were exactly what she herself intended to do.

But the girl was not going to be put off so easily. "Well, they *did* say he didn't even leave a note. That's queer if you ask me. Weren't there any clues at all?"

The housekeeper straightened up from the bed and shook her head in despair. "I suppose you'll get it from someone else if I don't tell you, since you seem determined to know. Of course, there isn't much to tell but . . ." She leaned over the bed and dropped her voice to a confidential whisper. ". . . there *were* the paw prints."

"Paw prints, m'um?"

"Yes, of a very large dog. They led all the way from the front door to this room, and then back out again. *But . . .*" Her voice dropped even lower and sounded as if she relished passing out this mysterious information after all. "... there was no dog to be found anywhere!"

"Didn't anyone see a dog come into the building?" the girl asked.

"No one!"

"Was there anything else?"

"Yes, one other thing, a very small yellow feather outside the door. I saw it myself," the housekeeper added importantly. "It was the feather of a tiny bird, but there was no bird to be found either!"

"Paw prints and a bird feather," the girl said. "Is that all?"

"I said there wasn't much," replied the housekeeper huffily. "Now let's get back to work, if you don't mind."

"Oh, I didn't mean it that way, m'um. Please," the girl pleaded, "I'd like ever so much to know more. What was the old gentleman like, to look at, I mean?"

"Like any other, I suppose," the housekeeper said with an indifferent shrug. But then she stopped her bed-making a moment to stare at the white sheet, an absent expression on her face. "Except there *were* those eyes of his."

"What about his eyes, m'um?"

"Remarkable they were, as if there wasn't anything they couldn't see."

"Oh!" breathed the girl.

The housekeeper drew her head back with a start, as if she had been caught napping. "Well, I don't know what all this has to do with anything. He's gone and he's gone, and it's all a great waste of time talking about him." She lifted up the last corner of the bed and drew the sheet under it with a determined snap. "Now, what's this?" she exclaimed as a folded piece of paper flew out from under the mattress and went floating downward.

The girl darted toward it, but not quickly enough, because the housekeeper's hand snatched it up just as it reached the floor. Yellowed with age, the paper crackled as it was unfolded. The housekeeper tried to guard it jealously, but the girl pressed up against her and peered around her shoulder so that she too saw the words penned in faded ink.

From *The Dictionary of Ancient Lore*—The Ninety-third Page

Furken—(Fur—abbreviated from the Middle English furren, meaning fur, plus ken [*sic*]—abbreviated from the Germanic kinder, meaning children.) The fur children. Descendents of a branch of the genus Elf, noted not only for their gaiety and fondness for dancing and singing, but also for their boldness, strength, courage, and their wildness and fierceness in battle. When, however, Humans began to take up the green spaces that once held Elfin kingdoms, the Furkens did not move on with other branches of Elves. For some unknown reason, they remained

and drifted into Human houses, which had sprung
up like giant mushrooms everywhere. Slowly, as
moss takes over a tree stump, the Furkens lost
their tang of Elf blood, and

"And what?" cried the girl as they reached the bottom of the page.

"How should I know?" said the puzzled and irritated housekeeper. "You can see as well as I that the writing has ended."

"But there's more on the back," the girl reminded her.

With maddening slowness, the housekeeper turned over the piece of paper. There, the writing continued.

they became soft, losing all their old glories and
along with them the tricks of the fairy folk. The most
important of these is the ability to vanish, the
trick of disappearing into thin air.

Gradually, over the centuries, the Furkens
changed in appearance. Coats of short, gray hair
now cover almost their entire bodies except for their
faces. Their eyes have become beady and sharp,
always looking out for danger. Their noses
have become long and pointed. For, having lost
their ability to vanish, they now use their noses like
animals to sniff out danger, as well as for a

quivering compass to point out food and shelter. In short, the Furkens have come to resemble what they hate most—the mice.

And here the words ended.

"Furkens!" breathed the girl excitedly. "Elves!"

"Mice!" whipped back the housekeeper with a shudder.

"Please, m'um, what are you going to do with the bit of paper? Might I have it?" the girl begged.

But the housekeeper thrust it firmly into the pocket of her voluminous brown apron. "Certainly not! It's only a bunch of nonsense, but I'll have to report it to the office at once. Mice!" she repeated grimly, and marched out of the room.

But the young girl remained, hands at her sides, staring with dreaming eyes at the rain washing down the windows, as if she half expected something, or someone, to appear.

The Barrel
IN THE *Basement*

ONE

Escape

"Tell him, Muddle! Tell him we're not mice!"

Pudding gazed with horror at the huge yellow cat who lay on his side daintily probing the mouth of the jar with his paw. Pudding pressed his back against the bottom of the jar, wishing that he and Muddle could disappear through it. But they couldn't. And the winter moon lit them up as clearly as an electric light would light up fish in a goldfish bowl.

Muddle's mouth opened and closed, but only gasps of air came out. His round, pudgy face was pale as washed sand. He opened his mouth wider. "Wha . . . wha . . . wha . . ."

The cat's claws swept past them with a whispering hiss of air.

"We're not mice!" Pudding burst out. "Go away . . . shoo, shoo!"

The cat looked surprised. His head tilted to one side as an eyebrow raised. Then a crafty grin spread across his face. "You don't say! Not mice?" He began to giggle. "Not mice? That's a good one!"

Dissolving into laughter, the cat rolled over on his back, waving his paws helplessly in the air. Tears rolled from his eyes, down his nose, and out to the tips of his whiskers, where they clung, frozen into pear-shaped diamonds. Finally, he quieted down enough to catch his breath. "You know something in there?" He thrust his nose as far into the jar as it would go. "They *all* say that!"

The tip of his tail began to twitch. "Look at you," he said, sneering, "short hair over most of you, beady black eyes, pointed nose and ears. Anyone who looks like you has to be mice."

"We don't have whiskers and tails!" said Pudding fiercely. "And when we're not rolling around in a jar, we don't walk on all fours!"

"So what!" said the cat. "I still say you're mice."

"We're no such thing!" cried Pudding. "We're . . ."

"Wha . . . wha . . . wha . . ." Muddle began once again.

"Who's that wha-wha-wha-ing?" asked the cat rudely.

"My friend, Muddle," replied Pudding. "He takes care of me."

The cat snickered. "Pity for you! I wish he'd be still. Anyway, if you're not mice, what are you?" He thrust his paw menacingly back into the jar.

Pudding drew in his breath to keep his voice from quivering. "We're Furkens."

"Whatkins?" asked the cat, his paw poised in midair.

"Furkens," replied Pudding. "We're a branch of Elves."

"Elves? You really are loony," said the cat.

"I'm not either," Pudding replied indignantly. "We *are* Elves!"

The cat's eyes widened slightly. "Do you think I'm an idiot? There's no such thing as an Elf. Everyone knows that."

"*We* don't know it!"

"Then you're cracked," replied the cat. "But just to show you how big-hearted I am, I'll let you prove what you are. Do something Elfy for me."

"Like what?" asked Pudding.

The cat rolled his eyes skyward, then leered into the jar. "Vanish!"

"I can't do that," Pudding replied quickly.

"Can *he*?"

"No, neither of us can. We've forgotten how. All Furkens have."

"Prune juice!" retorted the cat. "You never could do it, period. As far as I'm concerned, you and your fat friend are mice. After all, the true test of a mouse is in the smell, and you smell mighty mousey to me." The cat grinned slyly. "Look, if you really want to prove anything, come on out and let me have a close-up smell or two. I can soon tell if you're not one."

Smell mighty mousey to me! The words had no sooner left the cat's mouth than Pudding remembered something he'd all but forgotten, the mouseskin jacket he was wearing! Swiftly he pulled it off and hurled it through the mouth of the jar. It landed between the cat's paws.

The cat dropped one paw over the jacket and smashed it flat. A sudden look of surprise crossed his face, and for a moment he seemed too stunned to move. Then he sat up and began batting the limp mouseskin back and forth on the ground. After a few moments, he picked it up in his teeth, dropped it to the ground, and stared dumbly into the jar.

"There you are," said Pudding. "Do you know a mouse that's ever been able to peel off its skin?"

The cat shook his head.

"Now," Pudding swallowed hard, "put your nose as far into the jar as you can get it."

As if in a trance, the cat let the mouseskin jacket fall from his teeth and thrust his nose into the jar. In a moment, his whiskers began to twitch and his nose to wrinkle. Then his whole body shuddered as he quickly jerked his nose back out of the jar.

"What is that?" he muttered weakly.

"Warm apricot jam," replied Pudding. "It's the way Furkens smell. You can tell it when the mouse smell is gone."

"Whatkins?" said the cat.

"Elves," said Pudding. "We went through it all before."

"Oh yes, Elves!" said the cat. His voice seemed to be coming, like an echo, from the far-off tip of his tail. His eyes had begun to glaze over.

Just then, a voice called sharply through the frosty early morning air. "Marvin! Marvin!"

The cat's ears twitched slightly. He raised his head to listen, but with a distant air, as if he recognized the name, but wasn't entirely certain that it was his.

"Is that you?" Pudding asked.

The cat nodded slowly.

"Hadn't you better go?" Pudding suggested gently. "You might miss a good breakfast of tinned chicken and liver, maybe some warm milk. We'd only be a snack if you ever got to us. And Furkens taste the way they smell. We might make you ill."

The cat looked as if he was *already* ill as he struggled to his feet. For a few moments he stood staring down on the mouseskin at his feet, then he leaned over weakly and picked it up in his teeth. He started off in the direction of the voice. A few feet from the jar, he stopped, shook his head from side to side, and then continued on his way. He wobbled strangely as he walked.

"He's gone, Muddle!" Pudding cried as soon as he'd seen the cat disappear over the fence.

Muddle didn't seem to hear him at all. He stood stiff as an icicle, his mouth still frozen wide open as if he were about to make a speech.

Clinging as best he could to the sides of the slippery, curved glass, Pudding dragged the rigid Muddle down the length of the jar and out into the open. Then he began to shake his friend gently.

Color began to creep back to Muddle's plump face. His jaw began moving up and down.

"Wha . . . wha . . . wha . . . we're Furkens!" The words seemed almost to blow out of his mouth.

"It's all right, Muddle," Pudding said. "The cat's gone."

"Gone?" Muddle looked around helplessly. "Why so he has! By the great bearded moose, I don't know what happened to me. It must have been the cold glass. Like being frozen inside an ice cube. Everything went black before me."

Pudding shivered and drew his arms about himself. "What are we going to do now, Muddle?" he said. "It's almost daylight."

"I'll have to think of something," Muddle replied, and then added miserably, "if I can!" His face suddenly looked withered and gray, like an old potato.

"You've done very well so far, Muddle," Pudding told him.

This wasn't quite true, and Pudding knew it, considering the mess they were in. Muddle had somehow managed to get them from the country into the heart of the city. They had to hide by day in drain pipes and under cement steps littered with greasy papers and smelling of decayed garbage. Often they'd been frightened away from these second-rate hotel rooms by large, first-rate rats. They'd lost count of how many times they'd almost been killed by hurtling taxi cabs and lumbering buses.

"Well, we're really lost this time!" Muddle said. "We're cold and tired, and the food's all gone." He squeezed the rough little brown sack that hung limp and empty from his back. Days before, it had been plump with firethorn berries to serve as food for their journey.

"Look, Muddle!" Pudding grabbed his arm suddenly. "Aren't those houses over there? Why don't we try one of them?"

Muddle looked hopefully across the street, but shook his head at once. The moon shone over the roofs of a row of brick houses that stood so close together they seemed to be holding each other up. The sidewalk in front of them hid in shadows. But there was enough light to see that their front steps marched right down to the sidewalk.

"No gardens," Muddle said mournfully. "Not so much as a pea patch. Without gardens, where would we get food? Where would we get furnishings? Where would we *dance* at night?" Like a helpless child, he looked at

Pudding with a face ready to crumple into tears.

Even though it was Muddle who had found Pudding as a baby and cared for him all these years, sometimes Pudding felt twice as old as his friend. "We don't dance outdoors in the wintertime," he reminded Muddle, "not when it snows, at any rate. And besides, there might be gardens in the back. We ought to look. We can't stay here. The cat might be back."

"C . . . c . . . c . . . cat?"

"Come on, let's hurry!" Pudding said quickly. He gave Muddle's hand a tug and ran lightly across the empty street. With small, dry sounds of fear coming from his throat, Muddle trundled along behind him.

When they had reached the sidewalk that lay in shadows, Pudding began down it slowly, looking up at the tall houses that rose like brick giants over him. Suddenly he found himself going faster and faster. The dark sidewalk flew by under his feet.

"Wait up, Pudding!" gasped Muddle, as if all the air had been punched out of him.

Pudding hardly heard him. Directly in front of him, he had seen a wide slice of moonlight cutting between two houses and lying like a beacon on the pavement. A strange excitement crept over him. Looking back to make certain Muddle was following him, he darted between the houses.

Now he found himself running down a brick path toward a small gate that looked as if it was woven of gnarled driftwood. It seemed more to be growing than hanging from its rusted hinges. But the bricks under his feet were old and worn and slippery. He barely had time to look through the gate when behind him he heard Muddle crash to the ground and howl with pain. Pudding turned and ran swiftly back to where Muddle was lifting himself heavily off the ground.

"What is it? What's there?" Muddle grimaced as he rubbed his knees to see if anything was broken.

"It's a gate, Muddle, a gate to a garden!"

Muddle's face brightened. "A garden? A *real* one, Pudding?"

"A *beautiful* one, Muddle!"

"With trees?"

"Trees and everything! Come on, Muddle, come see for yourself." Pudding took Muddle's hand and pulled him toward the gate. Paying little attention to Muddle's gasps and groans, Pudding pushed him under it. Then the two of them stood and stared in silent wonder at the garden. It seemed, to Pudding at least, to be floating, entirely apart from the world, in its own magic pool of moonlight. It was almost as if it had been put there just for them.

"There *are* trees!" breathed Muddle.

"I said there were," Pudding told him. "And see what else, Muddle!"

"A . . . a blueberry!" Muddle lumbered to touch the bush to make sure it was real. "And a monstrous big

firethorn bush hugging the whole corner of the house."
He reached into it and pulled something off. "With big
fresh berries!"

"But look, Muddle, under that crabapple tree."
Pudding poked Muddle gleefully in the ribs. "*Moss!*"

"Dancing moss!" Muddle sounded as if he'd just
been sent a whole packet of new toys. His eyes sparkled.

But as he stood munching on a berry and staring at
the house, his round face suddenly turned ashen.

"What's wrong?" Pudding asked. It didn't seem to
him that anything in the world could be wrong now.

"Bricks are what's wrong, Pudding," Muddle said.
"Bricks! Look at them, solid right down to the ground.
We know there's a basement by the windows. But how
can we squeeze our way into it through bricks? And what
good is the garden to us if we can't live in the basement
of the house that goes with it?"

"But there must be a way in. There must!" Pudding
cried. It had begun to seem to him that everything that
had happened to them, the escape from their old home,
the whole terror-filled journey, had led them to this
place. It didn't seem possible that they were going to be
driven away by something so commonplace and ridiculous as bricks.

"Muddle!" he exclaimed suddenly. "Why couldn't
we stay here and live in a tree?"

"In a tree?" Muddle said dimly.

"Yes, in a tree," Pudding repeated excitedly. "We'd

have stairs going up inside the trunk, and little ledges, and windows looking out over all the garden. We could live in the tree the way Furkens used to when they were still proper Elves!"

At this, Muddle drew himself up stiffly. His chest swelled out and he pulled his two chins down into his neck so that suddenly three chins appeared. "We *are* still proper Elves!" he said.

But immediately after this performance, he drooped down, his chest collapsed, and his third chin retreated back into two. "We couldn't live in a tree," he said plaintively. "Who would build the house for us? And if we lived in it, what would protect us?"

Pudding knew that Muddle was right. Who would, and what would? Tears stung his eyes. "Will we have to leave, Muddle?"

In reply, Muddle looked at the sky, his face stiff with fear. "It's almost sunrise. We'll pick some firethorn berries before we look for a place to hide. But we'll have to hurry!"

There was nothing left to say. Silently they went to work.

Heavy, delicious clumps of berries hung close to the ground all around the bush. Gathering them was easy anywhere. But Pudding didn't want Muddle to see the tears glistening in his eyes. So he moved to the opposite side of the bush. It wasn't until he was certain that his tears had dried that he turned back toward his friend.

And it was then, where a shaft of moonlight pierced the thick bush, that he saw the thickest, plumpest cluster of all hanging against the house. The cluster shook as he picked a fat berry from it, and as it did, a tiny gleam of light shot out from the wall. Curiously, Pudding reached his hand to find out what was there.

The gleam came from a small lump, cold and smooth. Pudding snatched back his hand. It frightened him to feel the strange thing so suddenly. As his hand drew back, the moonlight fell on the lump once more, and an odd choked feeling rose in Pudding's throat: the lump was a tiny brass mushroom.

More than that, the mushroom was set in a door not five inches tall, not three inches across. It was exactly the right size for a mouse to scurry through. Or an Elf.

TWO

The Barrel in the Basement

"Muddle!" Pudding cried, excited and at the same time terrified by what he'd found.

Muddle's anxious face peered from around a clump of berries.

"I've found a door, a *real* one, Muddle! It's right in the bricks, and it's just our size," Pudding said.

Muddle drew nearer. "D . . . d . . . d . . . don't touch it, Pudding!" he shrieked suddenly.

"Why not?" Pudding asked. "It might be a way into the basement."

"That's not the question. The question is wh . . . wh . . . wh . . . who put it there! No mouse could build it. No Furken *would* do it and risk discovery. Who built it,

Pudding? Wh . . . wh . . . wh . . . who!" Muddle's jowls were quivering like soft jelly.

But even as Muddle spoke, the brass mushroom drew Pudding's hand like a magnet. Slowly he touched it. Slowly it turned in his hand, and the little door swung inwards. He took two steps into what seemed like a tunnel stretching out from the door. Behind him, Muddle groaned, but otherwise, for a moment, there was deadly silence in the tunnel. Then Pudding heard a small, whispering scratch of sound. It was so small that it was almost no sound at all. But Pudding knew that the darkness held *something*. He couldn't move. His heart thumped in his chest like a small bass drum, but his feet were frozen to the ground with terror.

Suddenly footsteps within the tunnel began marching firmly toward him. A moment later, a bright flash of light nearly blinded him. He squeezed his eyes shut, waiting to die. Then he slowly opened them.

In front of him stood a figure about Muddle's height, though much, much older, holding a tiny brass lantern in his hand. He wore a green leather jacket and a long red-and-white striped muffler around his neck. A little skirt of red, black, and white plaid came to just above his knees, which were knobby as two dimpled walnuts.

But Pudding wasn't nearly so much surprised by the clothing, the skirt in particular, as he was by the owner. "Y . . . you're a Furken!" he stammered.

"Hmmmmph!" snorted the old Furken. "If you'd been taught properly to use your nose for the pur-r-r-

poses of warning and protection as a Furken should, instead of merely as a thing of beauty, you would have recognized the smell of warm apricot jam at once!"

Pudding might ordinarily have laughed at the funny little skirt, the knobby knees, and the strange way the Furken had of rolling his r's when he talked. As it was, he was too frightened even to speak.

"Well,"—the Furken held his lantern up to Pudding's face—"I suppose when you've lived with your own pleasant scent for so long, it's not easy to pick up another one like it in a moment. Hmmmm." He moved the lantern closer. "I see you're only a boy." Then he looked suspiciously around Pudding. "Didn't I hear others with you?"

Pudding turned to see Muddle's face, pale as a turnip, peering out from behind the open door.

"It's all right, Muddle. He's a Furken!"

"A Furken?" Muddle stumped into the tunnel, scratching his head in amazement. "By the whirly-tailed elephant!"

"This is my friend, Muddle," Pudding said. "I live with him. My name is Pudding."

With this introduction, Muddle immediately rolled his eyes upwards, drew himself up stiff as a garden post, threw his hand to his chest with a huge thump, and finally made a deep bow. He went so far down that his sack, now filled with berries, nearly threw him over. "Pleased to meet you, I'm sure!"

The old Furken looked surprised, but managed a

curt bow in return. "Old Toaster," he said briefly. "What may I do for you?"

"We've managed to get ourselves a bit lost looking for a new home." The sad, gray expression on Muddle's face melted into a bright new one. "But it looks as if we might not have to look further!" He beamed at Old Toaster.

But Old Toaster's face had become as expressionless as a cup of milk. His eyes darted from Pudding to Muddle, and back to Pudding again. "Well," he said, "my quar-r-r-ters are big enough that I can put you up nicely for the day. However, though I don't wish to appear inhospitable, you'll have to be ready to go on your way tonight."

"On our way tonight?" said Muddle weakly.

Old Toaster shifted his feet uncomfortably. Then he shrugged and muttered, "It's nothing to do with me. Have you forgotten the Furken law?"

Muddle turned to Pudding. He looked as if the whole house had just fallen on his head. " 'One more than enough is too much.' " His voice shook. "I *had* forgotten it!"

So had Pudding, but he didn't have to be reminded of the reason for it. Because Furkens could so easily be mistaken in looks for mice, it was important to them not to behave like mice.

It was Muddle himself who had taught Pudding that when mice moved into a house, more mice moved in. Hundreds of mice with their mothers and fathers and

uncles and aunts and cousins twice and three times removed came to live. And they all had babies. In no time,
great clouds of chewing, scratching, smelly mice bal-
looned through a house. Furkens had made the law so
that this could never happen with them.

Still, who was to say how many were enough, and
what was too much? Three didn't seem like too much to
Pudding. It was clear that this Old Toaster simply didn't
want to share his basement. Why? And would Muddle ask
him? Pudding hoped desperately that he would.

But all Muddle did was draw himself up and fold
himself over into an even deeper bow than his first one.
"Yes, we do remember it now. It's quite right of you to
remind us, and very kind of you to let us stay with you for
the day."

Old Toaster cleared his throat as if to fill up the un-
happy silence. "Well, no sense in standing here in the
cold. Come on along with me and we'll see what can be
done to make you comfortable."

Holding the little brass lantern high over his head
to light the way, he started off down the tunnel, with
Muddle and Pudding trailing him in a silent procession.

From the tunnel, they stepped onto a narrow ledge over-
looking the basement. Pudding and Muddle exchanged
startled glances when they saw a neat miniature stairway

leading down to the floor. Without offering an explanation, Old Toaster led them down it. Then, still silent, he took them across the basement floor to a circle of light made by the furnace. In the center of the circle stood a large wooden barrel.

"But it's a house!" Pudding whispered to Muddle. Dumbly, Muddle nodded.

Little windows circled the barrel. From them hung deep brown shutters. Pudding looked up and saw a twisted tin chimney sending out a thin stream of soft gray smoke. And at the base of the barrel, a tiny brass mushroom blinked at him from a small arched door exactly like the one outside.

If this barrel had a bark covering, and if branches grew from it, Pudding told himself, it would be exactly like the kind of house where Furkens had lived when they were proper Elves! And when Old Toaster marshalled them through the small door, Pudding could see that the barrel was as much a proper Elf's house inside as out.

Four comfortable chairs of hollowed wood, with rough brown pillows on the seats, formed a cozy circle around a fireplace built of tiny gray pebbles. A fire crackled in the fireplace and sent bright sparks dancing onto the hearth.

Old Toaster pointed to the chairs. "Make yourselves comfortable," he said gruffly. "I'll get you something to eat."

Muddle and Pudding both dropped their sacks of berries on the floor with a thump, but only Muddle fell into a chair. Pudding remained standing with his back to the fire, his eyes on Old Toaster. There was something odd about this whole set-up.

Old Toaster went to work at once. From a sturdy oak cupboard he pulled out two polished walnut shells filled with sunflower seeds and thin strips of dried crabapple and a platter of pine bark on which lay a large dried black beetle. He set the shells and the platter on a table, which was a stump of wood cut from a tree branch, with smaller stumps drawn up to it. Finally, he drew water into a tiny stone pitcher from a wooden tap over a sink by the cupboard and set it on the table along with three acorn cups.

All the while he was doing this, he kept glancing over at the two in front of the fireplace. Law or no law, Pudding was certain that Old Toaster didn't want them there, and the sooner they left the better. And he especially didn't want Pudding there. His eyes hardly left Pudding for a moment.

When his preparations were completed, Old Toaster beckoned to them. "Supper's ready," he announced with a curt nod.

Muddle's eyes roamed over the table hungrily as they drew up their chairs. "I see you follow the custom of eating only Elf food as we still do," he said. "As I've taught my young friend, Pudding, here, it's one thing we can still do to keep from being totally de-Elfinized."

"Of course," said Old Toaster briefly.

Pudding noticed that his beetle leg was dusty, and a great deal drier than even dried beetle ought to be. His crabapple strip was so tough he could hardly chew it, as if it had been sitting on the shelf for a very long time. But he said nothing and tried to swallow his supper the best way he could.

As they munched and crunched on their supper, Muddle seemed to be drumming up the courage to ask Old Toaster a question, and he finally managed it. "The tunnel, the . . . er . . . stairs, and . . . and all this"—he pointed around the barrel—"you did it all yourself?" His voice brimmed over with awe.

Old Toaster only grunted and shrugged as if to say it wasn't so much to do.

"And nobody's come after you . . . the Humans who live in this house . . . living out in the open like this?"

"No one has yet," Old Toaster replied coolly. Taking a sip of water from his acorn cup, he never spilled a drop.

It was certain that Old Toaster didn't want to waste any extra words on them. He answered Muddle's questions briefly, or didn't answer them at all. He asked very few questions himself. It was a silent, uncomfortable supper party, and Pudding was glad when it was over.

The table quickly cleared, Old Toaster then threw open the cover of a miniature seaman's chest by the front door and began pulling out armloads of soft, dry leaves. These he formed into beds before the fireplace. When they had been arranged to his satisfaction, he pointed to two of them. "Those are for you," he said. "Now I'll wish you a good day. I'll wake you at the pr-r-r-oper time in the evening."

After this, he carefully removed his long muffler, stepped out of his skirt, folded them both and laid them neatly on the floor by his bed. Then he turned down the flame in the brass lamp, collapsed onto the leaves, and appeared to go off to sleep at once. But Pudding, who lay curled up under an oak leaf, was certain that all the time he really had one eye a crack open, watching.

For a long time, Pudding couldn't fall asleep. He lay listening to the leaves crackle as Muddle tossed restlessly in his bed. But after a while, Muddle grew quiet, and then his snores began. It was a comfortable, familiar sound to Pudding. With each shuddering snore, the chair beside him rattled a reply. Shudder, rattle! Shudder, rattle! The chorus finally lulled him to sleep.

It was a restless sleep in which he dreamed he was being blown across an ice-covered pond by a bitter wind. But even though the wind blew him and blew him, he could never quite reach the other side.

He woke up shivering. The oak leaf had fallen off him, and there was little left of the fire in the fireplace but gray ashes. He pulled the oak leaf back up under his chin and looked across at Muddle. Muddle's snores had become a quieter bubble-whish, bubble-whish, but he was still sleeping heavily. Then Pudding looked toward Old Toaster's bed.

The muffler was gone. The skirt was gone. And Old Toaster was gone!

A moment later Pudding climbed out of his bed, opened the little door, and stepped softly out of the barrel into the basement.

§🐌

A clear, wintry, late-afternoon sun now poured through the windows. Soon Old Toaster would be back to waken them. Pudding knew that if he was going to do any investigating, it would have to be done quickly. He started toward the little stairway they had come down earlier, and then made a remarkable discovery. Directly to his left was a second stairway exactly like the first one!

Pudding hesitated, and then turned and crept toward it. Swiftly, two at a time, he ran up the steps. He was met at the top by a tightly shut Human door. But at the bottom of the door was set another door, as if there were a very tiny cat or dog in the house who was allowed to come in and out of the basement at will. It was identical to the small arched doors with brass mushroom handles that Pudding had seen twice before! He grabbed the mushroom. It turned in his hands, and the door swung open.

Sunlight streamed through a wide window onto a red checkered cloth spread over a kitchen table. A bright copper teakettle hummed softly on a stove. The room was warm and inviting, but it was empty.

Across the brick-colored linoleum floor, Pudding saw a large brown earthenware dish marked "DOG" in bold white letters. Dogs were safe. He didn't need to worry about that. Quickly he scanned the rest of the floor for smaller dishes with bits of smelly leftover fish glued to them or little saucers of cream that meant "cat." To his relief, there were none. But it was then that he saw the bright flash of light at the bottom of the closed door on the far side of the kitchen. He ran toward it, and it was just as he expected, another tiny brass mushroom on another small arched door! Did the doors go all through the house? he wondered. He stretched out his hand toward the mushroom.

Suddenly, he began to wish he had wakened Muddle. Now he was all alone in the heart of a Human house where at any moment giant feet might thunder into the room, a loud voice shriek, "Mouse!" and a broom crash down over his head or, worse yet, a shower of scalding water from the kettle now steaming peacefully on the stove.

But even as he stood wondering if he shouldn't run back to the safety of the basement, his trembling hand was being drawn toward the mushroom. As if he were in a dream, it turned in his hand, and the door opened.

Now he was in a room where the sun gleamed softly off a polished cherry table and six chairs. It made a pattern of shadows on the blue rug beneath it. That room was empty, too, but from across it, another pinprick of light flashed back at Pudding from another arched door. And from behind this door there came voices!

Over the rug, soft as cornsilk, Pudding ran to the door. His heart thudding so hard in his chest it almost crushed out his breath, he reached out a shaking hand toward the mushroom. It turned in his hand. And the door opened.

THREE

One More than Enough

In a room lined with bookshelves that stretched from floor to ceiling, two well-worn green leather chairs were drawn up before a fire that leaped up the chimney of a stone fireplace.

A Man sat in one chair. His feet, in scuffed red slippers with both toes out, were propped on a low, round oak table buried under a mountain of books and papers. The Man's feet were at the end of such long, thin legs they hardly seemed to belong to him at all. From time to time, he raked his fingers through the gray hair that stood out from his head like a mop of steel wool.

On the floor, under the Man's legs, which formed a bridge across to the table, lay a huge great Dane with his head drooped across his paws. He seemed to be asleep.

And on the second chair, seated on the front of the cushion, leaning comfortably back against the arm, complete with striped muffler and plaid skirt, was Old Toaster!

On his feet, stretched in front of him, he now wore a pair of scuffed red slippers. Except for the size, they were exactly like those the man wore, including the holes in the toes. In his hand, he held a silver cup about one half the size of a small thimble.

Except for the crackling of the fire, the room was silent. Both the man and Old Toaster seemed to be in deep thought. The dog, like a limp gray mountain, slept. No one had noticed the little door open.

Pudding was too stunned to move. How could Old Toaster be sitting there with a Man? he asked himself. Elf history told of a time when some Humans "talked with the Little People," and had dealings with Elves. But no such story had ever been told about Furkens, especially not since they'd changed so much. To a Human, a Furken not only looked like a mouse, he sounded like one. There was no such thing as conversations or friendly meetings between Humans and Furkens. The idea was so ridiculous that no one had even invented a myth about it.

Suddenly, the huge dog's eyelids began to quiver. He stiffened and began to whine. Pudding quickly snapped the little door shut. Then he cautiously reopened it a crack, just enough to allow one eye to peek through. The dog stood up, sniffing the air.

"What is it, Thor?" the Man asked. "What's the matter, old boy?"

Thor studied the room anxiously and whined again.

"There's no one here. Just Old Toaster and me," the Man said reassuringly.

Almost as if he understood the words, the dog lumbered over to Old Toaster and sniffed further. Old Toaster looked annoyed and drew up his feet.

"There, you see?" said the Man. "Now come back here and settle down."

The dog thumped back again, put his head down on his master's lap, and allowed his ear to be rubbed. His tail began to wave slowly back and forth like a windshield wiper. In a few moments, he dropped to the ground and lowered his great jowls over his paws with a tired sigh.

"Wonder what's wrong with him?" the Man said.

Old Toaster grunted. "You've been feeding him too much! I told you he didn't need those biscuits at noon. If you ask me, Noah, you're stuffing him to death." As he spoke, Old Toaster popped what looked to Pudding like a small cracker spread with cheese into his mouth.

The Man, Noah, smiled. "I'll try to mend my ways," he said. He adjusted himself comfortably in his chair. "Now, have I given you long enough to think through my proposal?"

Old Toaster scowled at the ceiling. "You're making it very difficult for me, Noah. You know how a Furken feels about the Law. Even *they* didn't put up any argument. Not a word!"

"No, they wouldn't!" Noah looked distinctly annoyed. "Excuse me for saying so, Toaster, but you Furkens are all too blasted polite if you want to know. I'd have put up a token resistance, at least."

"Well, you're not a Furken!" said Old Toaster coldly. He jumped up and started for the little ladder that stood against his chair.

"No, I'm not. And I—" Noah stopped. "Where are you going?"

"To bed!"

Noah ran his fingers through his hair, making it a wilder mop than ever. "Look, Toaster, I'm sorry for what I said. I didn't mean it. You know that. We've never had a quarrel before."

"*They're* the ones who did it. They haven't been here a day and look what's happened."

"All that's happened is that I made an unthinking remark, for which I'm sorry. Don't go off angry, Toaster!"

Old Toaster hesitated. Then, without a word, he returned to his seat.

"Thank you!" Noah said simply.

"Don't mention it!" Old Toaster replied. After several moments, he grunted. "But I still say no more than two Furkens to a house!"

Noah curled his long legs up and over Thor, stood up, and strode to a bookshelf. He pulled down a large gray book. It appeared to be very old; its binding hung from it in shreds. He began thumbing eagerly through its tattered pages.

"Here . . . here it is!" He pointed a long, thin finger halfway down a page. " 'One more than enough is too much.' That's the law!"

"So?" questioned Old Toaster. "I already know that."

"Well, who ever determined what was 'enough'?"

"I still say two's plenty," grumbled Old Toaster.

"See here, let's forget the law for a moment and consider the other factors." Noah thrust the book back onto the shelf and returned to his chair. "They're lost in the city. They might freeze to death before they found a place around here to move into."

"Then help them to find a farm like the one they said they came from."

"How do you propose we do that?"

"Put them in the car and take them to the country," replied Old Toaster indifferently.

"You mean just drop them off someplace in the middle of nowhere? Toaster, I'm surprised at you!"

"Well, I'm surprised at you, too," said Old Toaster tartly. "Wanting to spoil the nice arrangement we have here. All you want is just a *collection* of Elves. You're not fooling me!"

Noah laughed. "I'll have to admit the thought crossed my mind. But see here, Toaster, it *is* the dead of winter. I don't believe you'd let me take *kittens* and dump them in the country, or leave them on someone's doorstep. These are Furkens . . . *Furkens*, Toaster . . . your own kind. Just think about it!"

Old Toaster jumped up, and with his hands clasped behind his back, he began pacing up and down the front of his chair. His skirt swung determinedly from side to side.

Suddenly he stopped and faced Noah. "There's something else!"

"I rather thought so," Noah said. "Well, what else?"

"The boy . . . the one called Pudding."

"Oh, so that's it! Well, what's wrong with Pudding?"

Old Toaster frowned. "I don't tr-r-r-rust him! Who do you think found the door to the tunnel? Why he's probably snooping around the basement right now! If they stay here, he'll discover my arrangement with you in no time at all, and the next thing, the peacefulness of this house will go right up the chimney with the smoke!"

"Nonsense! I won't let it," Noah said.

"I don't want them to know about us at all!"

"They won't from me!" Noah promised. "Tell them they must stay in the basement just as I'm certain they always have. Make them promise never to meddle in the second door leading from it. As for me, I'll ignore the barrel when I come down. They'll think I'm very stupid, but it won't bother me."

Old Toaster rubbed his chin thoughtfully. "How about living arrangements. I like my privacy, you know. Where would they live?"

"Why in the attic of the barrel, of course!" replied Noah without a moment's hesitation. "There's space for an entire apartment up there. I'll take care of the whole thing, just as I have the rest."

At this remark, Old Toaster stiffened. Then he cleared his throat several times before speaking. "I've . . . er . . . led them to believe I've done it all myself, the stairs, the barrel and the rest."

"They'll never know otherwise," Noah broke in quickly. "I assure you I'll manage the whole thing quite secretly."

"I've also . . . er . . . led them to believe I dine solely on . . . er . . . Elf food." Old Toaster's face had by now turned a bright red.

Noah smiled. "Well then, you'll just have to eat a little less up here and a little more down there. A fresh firethorn berry now and then instead of strawberry tart wouldn't hurt you a bit, Toaster. So how about it? Is it agreed?"

Once more, Old Toaster began marching up and down the chair. His muffler swung furiously back and forth. "I must think over what you've said."

Noah grinned and calmly picked up a pocket knife and a tiny stick from the table. He began scraping the stick with the knife.

Curious, Old Toaster stopped midway across the chair. "What's that?"

"Your new cane. Here, try it for size." Noah rose and handed Old Toaster the little stick.

"Hmmmmph!" snorted Old Toaster. "Thought you'd forgotten all about it."

"No, I was just waiting to find the right piece of burled walnut. Do you like it?"

"It's very handsome," Old Toaster said gruffly. "Well . . ."

"Well?"

"Well, you've won out, of course. They can stay!"

"You old rogue, I thought you'd agree to it!" exclaimed Noah. "Let's shake on it." He bent over, took Old Toaster's hand gently with his right thumb and forefinger, and the two shook hands solemnly.

They never heard the little door with the mushroom handle softly closing.

FOUR

The Second Door

"By the fuzzy-winged hippopotamus!" said Muddle, sleepily rubbing his eyes. "You're certain you saw all that, Pudding. You didn't dream it?"

"Of course I didn't, Muddle!" Pudding said indignantly. "See for yourself. Old Toaster's bed is empty, isn't it? He's upstairs right now talking to the Man."

"Talking to the Man . . ." Muddle's voice drifted off. "Talking to the Man!" He repeated the words slowly as if he were carving them on his brain. "But there's no such thing as talking to a Man!" His head waved helplessly from side to side. "You're not making this all up to fool old Muddle, are you, Pudding?"

"I wouldn't do that, Muddle. You know I wouldn't! I tell you I *heard* it. I *saw* it *all*!"

"And the Man said we could stay?"

"He *wants* us to, Muddle. He told Old Toaster so. He persuaded Old Toaster that we should. And it's just as I said. The Man is going to make an apartment for us in the attic of the barrel!"

"An apartment in the attic of the barrel just for us! Furniture perhaps . . . chairs . . . an oak cupboard for storing food . . . a small stone pitcher for gathering morning dew!" Muddle's eyes filled with tears. "No more scurrying behind boxes! No more hiding under chests!"

"But Muddle," Pudding said, "remember that we're not to know any of this."

"Don't worry," Muddle said, "I'll remember it!" Suddenly he began to smile. His smile broadened.

"What's funny?" Pudding asked.

"Making us think he's done all this himself! Letting us believe he's so brave he'd live right out in the open without fear of anyone! Why, he's just as helpless and scared as any Furken. He's . . . why, he's no better than I am!"

Pudding plopped down on the leafy bed beside Muddle and dug him in the ribs. "You should have seen him stuffing his face with crackers and cheese, Muddle. And the man says he eats strawberry tart!" Pudding giggled.

"Strawberry tart!" exclaimed Muddle. "No wonder he had such a limp appetite at supper. I noted it. Still, I don't blame him. The food did have a peculiar *ancient* taste about it."

"My beetle leg had dust on it," said Pudding, making a face. "I ate it to be polite. You know, Muddle, I believe he keeps Elf food in his cupboard just to fool surprise visitors like us."

"Or to fool himself," said Muddle. "I admit I don't entirely dislike him for all his gruff ways, but he's an old fraud just the same!" A few moments passed, and then Muddle repeated the word, "Fraud!" as if he liked the sound of it.

"An old fraud!" echoed Pudding. He dug Muddle in the ribs.

Muddle dug him back, and they began to laugh. They sat on the bed laughing and howling with glee over their discovery until suddenly Muddle's head snapped up.

"Ssssst, Pudding, he's coming back! He mustn't know we've been talking."

Pudding leaped into his bed.

By the time Old Toaster walked through the door into the barrel, Pudding had his oak leaf drawn snugly up under his chin, and his eyes shut, and Muddle's fake snores were shaking the barrel so mightily it seemed as if the ceiling would fall down on all of them.

"So you see," said Old Toaster, "I have decided that nowhere in the law does it state that three is too many." He coughed importantly. "Or even four, for that matter. So if you wish to stay, I suppose there's no reason why you shouldn't."

He was standing before the fireplace, his hands behind his back, solemnly addressing Muddle and Pudding, who were sitting, almost like two naughty schoolchildren, in chairs in front of him.

"That's very fine of you," Muddle said, managing to sound as if this was the very first time he'd heard the news. "I don't know what we would have done if we'd had to go on."

"Well, you don't have to worry about that now," returned Old Toaster grandly. "As for living arrangements, you can see by the ladder there next to the cupboard that there is a room over this one, an attic. It can be finished nicely into an apartment. We'll have steps going up the barrel on the *outside*, however," he added pointedly. "The upstairs apartment will be yours. *This* will be *mine!*"

"Oh, of course!" Muddle assured him. Then he looked slyly at Pudding. "But who is going to build all this?"

"Oh, I'll take care of it," said Old Toaster quickly. "Er . . . while you're sleeping. I would *prefer* that you didn't do a thing."

"That's splendid of you," said Muddle. "But are you certain you want no help? Pudding and I—"

"*Quite* certain!" interrupted Old Toaster firmly.

Frowning, he turned to stare into the fireplace as if he had to run through all these weighty matters in his mind.

Behind Old Toaster's back, Muddle rolled his beady black eyes around in his head and then winked mischievously at Pudding. "How will we manage food?" he asked. "*Elf* food."

Old Toaster started. "Oh yes, Elf food, of course." It took him a moment to collect his thoughts on the subject. "As for that, everything you will need you'll find in the garden; nuts, berries, and seeds."

"Caterpillars too?" inquired Muddle.

"Caterpillars?" repeated Old Toaster blankly. It was easy to see that he hadn't thought about the subject in a very long time.

"For roasting," explained Muddle.

"For roasting, of course!" Old Toaster mumbled. "Splendid caterpillars for roasting . . . er . . . in the spring."

Pudding could hardly keep from laughing. Muddle sent him another twinkling glance. "The Human, the Man you say lives here, hasn't he ever been curious about the barrel? Doesn't he ever come prying?"

"I said you don't have to worry about him," Old Toaster replied crossly. "The one thing you have to worry about is never to open the second door from the basement."

"The second door?" said Muddle, looking surprised.

"There is a second door, our size, that leads into the

house," said Old Toaster. "It's there for . . . er . . . emergency purposes. You are never to open it!"

"And what if we did?" asked Muddle.

Old Toaster stiffened. "I should be forced to ask you to leave!"

There was no mistaking the tone of his voice. The games and the fun-making had ended. Muddle turned pale as an oyster. "Do you hear that?" he said to Pudding in a voice beginning to quiver. "We're never to open the second door!"

Pudding nodded meekly and was glad that Old Toaster hadn't asked him if he already *had* opened it!

Even before the furniture appeared, while there was nothing but the piles of leaves he and Muddle slept on, Pudding grew to love their room in the attic of the barrel. From the tiny window over his bed he could see two old blue steamer trunks with faded labels peeling from them, crates filled with books, a pair of worn garden boots still caked with dried summer mud, shovels and rakes stacked in a corner waiting for spring, and rows of paint tins across a shelf with paint brushes hanging below them like animal's tails. A workbench littered with screwdrivers, hammers, nails, wood shavings, and sawdust fascinated Pudding.

The stairs leading up the outside of the barrel to the

new apartment, and all the furnishings, appeared with remarkable ease and swiftness. And it all happened, just as Old Toaster had said it would, while Muddle and Pudding were asleep. Or at least while they were *supposed* to be asleep. As Muddle's snores thundered through the barrel, Pudding often crept to his window and peeked out at the Man, Noah, stealthily making the small furniture at his workbench.

More often than not, Old Toaster was just as sound asleep as Muddle while all this took place, and Noah tiptoed to the barrel with his newly finished cupboard or chair, leaving it at Old Toaster's front door like Santa Claus delivering his secret toys. He never failed to smile gently down on the barrel, sometimes patting it and saying, "Sleep well, little Elf friends!" before he returned upstairs. Without ever meeting Noah, Pudding loved him dearly.

However, though it was no time at all before they got down to the business of everyday living, Old Toaster remained aloof. They might be neighbors sharing apartments in the same barrel, but he did not take this to mean that they needed to share secrets as well. Whatever questions Pudding or Muddle had about the never-heard-of-before arrangement between a Furken and a Man would never be answered, it seemed.

"I don't understand why he won't even dance with us!" Muddle said plaintively one crisp cold night when a clear moon shone invitingly down on the garden.

"Why don't we ask him just this once more?" Pudding said as they were going down the steps of the barrel from their apartment. "He might this time."

Muddle sighed. "Once more," he said, and knocked on Old Toaster's door.

But Old Toaster was no more inclined to dance with them on this night than on any other.

"Thank you all the same," he said stiffly. "Too cold."

"You'll warm with the dancing!" Pudding offered helpfully.

"Bones ache," replied Old Toaster.

Muddle shuffled his feet uncomfortably. "Won't you ever dance with us?" he asked.

"Haven't danced in years," Old Toaster said gruffly. "Too old to start now. Was there anything else?"

Muddle and Pudding shook their heads, and Old Toaster unceremoniously shut the door with a firm click.

"Too old has nothing to do with it, do you think, Muddle?" Pudding stepped through the tunnel door into the garden. "He just doesn't want to be friends."

"I believe you're right," Muddle returned, "but it doesn't keep us from dancing. And tonight we will!" He looked searchingly at the sky. His nose twitched as he sniffed the air. "Tomorrow there'll be snow on the moss, Pudding. So tonight we'll make the most of it!"

They hurried to their favorite patch of soft, spongy moss under the crabapple tree. There, they took one another's hands to form a circle and, with toes pointed, began at once to move slowly round as Pudding sang, in a high flutelike voice, the words Muddle had taught him.

> *"Slowly, slowly, we begin,*
> *Moon touch sun close earth within.*
> *Right to bend, then left to bend,*
> *No beginning, never end.*
> *Forest moss touch Elfin toes,*
> *Through needle leaves the song wind flows.*
> *Faster, faster, round and round,*
> *The mushroom grows without a sound.*
> *Darkling spaces never bare,*
> *Elfin toes everywhere.*
> *Spin, spin, spin!"*

Whirling, dipping, spinning, they danced for hours.

When Pudding finally fell into bed, his brain went right on spinning like a dandelion seed blowing in the wind. Once, while they were dancing, he was certain he'd seen Old Toaster's face peek suddenly from around the tunnel door, but it had disappeared just as suddenly. Why, Pudding wondered, did Old Toaster continue to keep them at such a distance? Would they never have their questions answered about him and Noah?

Pudding couldn't drop off to sleep; and finally he threw back his oak leaf coverlet and stood staring out his window. Lantern light still streamed from Old Toaster's windows below, but soon it dimmed and went out. Muddle had long since begun to snore.

Until now, Pudding had carefully kept away from

the forbidden door. Muddle, terrified that they would be asked to leave, warned time and again that he must never open it. But tonight, Pudding felt that he must look at it up close once more. He would just look at it, he told himself, perhaps touch the mushroom handle. He would not open it.

Silently, he crept from the room down the stairs and, a few moments later, had passed the trunks, the garden boots, and a heap of sweet-smelling sawdust on the floor. His footsteps made no sound at all as he moved stealthily up the staircase. And the doorway was there just as it always had been, but the door itself was wide open! Moonlight gleamed on the linoleum floor of the kitchen. It lit up the dog's dish and one leg of the table. Pudding crept closer to it.

Suddenly, as if a black curtain had dropped over it, the kitchen scene was cut off. A strong, warm, moist draft whistled through the doorway. Pudding clutched the stair railing and hung there, trembling. The warm air sucked in and out and nearly tore his arm off. By now Pudding recognized the black curtain as being a very large animal nose.

"Toaster?" a voice growled. "I know you're there. What are you doing wandering around at this hour. I hope you're not going to wake Master!"

The black nose withdrew from the doorway, and a large, drooping eye appeared in its place.

"Oh, I see it's not Toaster. You must be one of the new ones. Which one are you?"

"I . . . I . . . I . . ." stammered Pudding.

"Speak up," the deep voice said gently. "It's all right."

"I'm Pudding."

"The boy?"

Pudding nodded.

"Well, I can understand why you don't want to admit it. I suppose you know Old Toaster is very nervous about you. But don't worry. I won't reveal a thing. I'm very dependable along those lines as you'll come to find out." The eye withdrew from the doorway. "Why don't you come closer? You can let go of the railing. I won't blow you off, I promise."

Pudding let his hands slip away from the railing, and he inched closer to the door.

"By the way, I forgot to introduce myself. I'm Thor, the house dog. Are you afraid of dogs?"

Pudding shook his head.

Thor heaved a great sigh. "That's good. Old Toaster's scared witless of me. He thinks I'm going to step on him and squash him flat, but I'd never do that. I may look big and clumsy, but I can be light on my feet as a ballet dancer. However, I'm kept out of the basement on Toaster's account. Look, couldn't you step through the door a few inches? I'm getting a stiff neck trying to talk to you through that idiotic little hole."

"I can't," said Pudding.

"Why not?"

"We had to promise Old Toaster never to open this door, and I promised it," said Pudding.

"So you've kept your promise. You didn't open it. Did you make any promises about not stepping through the door if someone was stupid enough to leave it open?"

"No," said Pudding.

"Well, then, I don't see how any jury could convict you if you did. It seems like a clear case of open and shut to me, or vice versa. Come on in and let's make ourselves comfortable. I have a few questions I'd like to have answered."

Pudding hesitated. "I guess I have a few questions I'd like to have answered myself," he said, and stepped through the door.

FIVE

Explanations

"So it *was* you outside the door that night!" Thor said.

"If you knew, why did you give up trying to find me?" Pudding asked. He was stretched out on the linoleum, leaning against the brown bowl marked "DOG."

Thor yawned. "Kindness! And besides, I didn't want to give Old Toaster the satisfaction of being right about you. I happen to like boys."

"And I happen to like dogs," said Pudding.

A nice, comfortable silence fell in the kitchen.

"Why was it you had to leave the house in the country?" Thor asked.

"It was being sold. We overheard the Humans talking. They were going to build lots of small houses all over where the big house had been."

"Couldn't you have moved into one of those?"

"They said there weren't going to be any basements. There would just be cement. Living under a block of cement wouldn't be very comfortable."

"It doesn't sound too cozy," Thor said. He scratched his ear lazily. "But why didn't you wait until spring to leave?"

"We were going to," Pudding replied, "but the Humans moved out, and the rats moved in. We're deathly afraid of rats. We're deathly afraid of everything. We're the worst kind of cowards."

Thor grunted sympathetically. "Don't you have any kind of weapons to protect yourselves . . . sharp teeth, claws, anything like that?"

Pudding shook his head. "We used to have a kind of weapon, but that was thousands of years ago. It was nothing you could see or feel. It was nothing you had to carry around with you. Nobody even knew you had it. It was the very best kind of protection in the world."

"What was it?" Thor asked curiously.

"We could vanish," said Pudding. "We could disappear into thin air."

"Just like that?"

"Just like that!" said Pudding.

"What happened?" Thor asked. "Why can't you vanish now?"

"When Humans began to fill up the green places, lots of Elves moved away, but Furkens stayed and moved into Human basements. They counted on Human houses to protect them from storms, animals, goblins . . . things

like that. They grew lazy and didn't worry about protecting themselves anymore. And in the end they forgot how to vanish."

"What did they do when there was danger?"

"The same thing we do now," Pudding said, "run and hide, just like mice. That's when they began to look like mice, too, with the short hair, pointed noses, and all the rest. We try to do as many Elf things as we can, like eat Elf food, but it doesn't do any good. We're still scared Furkens. We'll never be proper Elves again." Pudding stared at the floor. When he looked up at Thor, tears trembled on his lashes. "I hate being a Furken!"

"You shouldn't feel that way," Thor said gently. "You shouldn't hate being what you are."

"Well, I do," said Pudding. "We all do, even if we don't say so. Even our names are soft and cowardly. How would you like to be called Muddle or Pie-flake or Slipper. Or Pudding! I hate being Pudding. It sounds so . . . so spongy!"

Thor looked startled. "Who are Pie-flake and Slipper? I thought there were just two of you?"

"There are now. They were my mother and father."

"Were?"

"They were killed," Pudding said simply.

"I'm sorry," said Thor. "How did it happen?"

"We're not certain. Muddle knew them, and he says Pie-flake was always trying to vanish. He and Slipper went walking in the forest one day, and there was danger. Muddle says he thinks Pie-flake tried to vanish instead of hiding. So he and Slipper were killed. I was riding in a walnut shell on Slipper's back. The shell fell over me. Muddle heard me crying under it and found me. The walnut shell saved me and kept me from being killed too."

"That's a very sad story," Thor said. "Have . . . have *you* ever tried to vanish?"

"Lots of times," Pudding replied. "I had to stop because it worried Muddle."

"I don't blame him. But how would you go about trying to vanish . . . I mean, if you wanted to." Thor asked.

"Muddle told me that Pie-flake said you close your eyes, hold your breath, and wish you weren't a Furken. But it didn't work for him. I guess it's never worked for anyone. I haven't tried it in ages."

"Just as well," said Thor.

Pudding sighed. "But how I wish I could vanish! I want to be a proper Elf again. I want to be brave. Just think, we could wander about in the daylight and never be afraid of Humans, or rats, or cats, or . . ."

Thor's ears quivered. "Cats?"

"Yes, we're almost as afraid of them as rats. They leave us alone once they get a smell of us, but sometimes they pounce before they smell. It's happened more than once."

Suddenly, Thor grinned. "That wasn't your little group that had the run-in with a cat named Marvin, was it? He lives across the street."

Pudding shuddered. "Yes, it was. He chased us into a glass jar. It was terrible. Is he your friend?"

"Yes and no," said Thor, and began to chuckle. A moment later, he was shaking with silent laughter. His tail banged helplessly on the floor. At last, he was able to control himself enough to go on talking. "Marvin always makes fun of me because I'm kept in the yard and only allowed out on a leash. He sits on the fence and hoots and hollers at me. He thinks he's cock of the walk. But you should see him now, weaving around like an idiot. He really looks ill. He keeps talking about those 'whatkins' he saw, how they peel off their skins, smell like warm apricot jam, and insist they're Elves. He looks awful. His mistress is making him take lots of terrible-tasting medicine. Serves him right!"

"Haven't you told him about us?" Pudding asked.

"Why should I? Let him suffer a little," Thor replied.

"Doesn't he know about Old Toaster?"

"Not a thing. I keep that cat out of the yard. He may laugh at me, but when I growl, he scats. Old Toaster is Master's and my little secret." Thor stretched and gave a shuddering yawn. "Well, I'm getting tired. Why don't you run along home so we can both get some sleep?"

"But we've only answered *your* questions. How about mine?" complained Pudding.

"Oh, you can come back tomorrow," Thor said easily.

"The door might be closed!"

Thor grinned. "Don't worry. It won't be. My paws may look big and clumsy, but they can perform some very dainty tasks."

"Like opening little doors?" said Pudding.

"Among other things," said Thor.

&

"Now what was it you wanted to know?" asked Thor. It was the following night, and once he was certain that Old Toaster and Muddle were asleep, Pudding had returned to the kitchen.

"I want to know about your master," Pudding replied promptly.

"What would you like to know about him?"

"Everything," said Pudding.

Thor sighed. "Well, his name is Noah Ebenezer Bender. He used to be a lawyer. He's retired from work now. When he came to live in this house, he got me to be his dog. He's the best master in the world. He doesn't treat me as if I were stupid. He believes I understand everything he says. Every time he leaves the house, he takes me with him. We don't always eat on time, but our between-the-meals are splendid. I lead a very good life. I'm a happy dog!" Thor sat looking dreamily at the refrigerator.

"Is that all?" asked Pudding.

Thor looked surprised. "What else is there?"

"Lots of things," said Pudding. "To begin with, how did he meet Old Toaster? Was Old Toaster already in the house when Noah came here?"

"Oh no!" Thor exclaimed. "Master brought him back from a journey he made to a land way across the ocean."

"Is that why Old Toaster dresses so funny?" Pudding asked. "Do they dress that way in the place where Noah found him?"

"You mean the skirt?" Thor chuckled. "Yes, I suppose they do. Toaster didn't dress that way at first. It was when he got homesick that Master made him the skirt."

"Did Old Toaster *want* to leave his home and come with Noah?" Pudding asked.

"Oh, yes! Noah wouldn't have brought him otherwise. I'm surprised Toaster wasn't too scared to make the journey, though, but he did it. He really likes Noah."

"But how did they start talking? How can Noah understand Old Toaster? How can they have conversations?" In his eagerness, Pudding ran all the questions together.

"Whoa! Slow down a minute!" Thor stood up, stretched, and collapsed again into a relaxed lumpy heap on the floor. "I'm afraid I can't answer all those questions. Master has always believed in Elves, he tells Old Toaster. Maybe that's how it happened. Funny thing, I don't think he was surprised about it. I think he expected to find an Elf one day and talk with him."

"But we sound like mice," said Pudding. "It isn't even the same thing."

"There's no accounting for magic," said Thor dreamily.

Silence fell in the kitchen.

"You haven't told me about the barrel yet," Pudding said at last.

"Master's idea. Old Toaster thought he shouldn't go so far as to live in the house, but Master wanted him to live in comfort and style. He thought up the idea of the barrel. The little doors through the house are his idea, too."

"I thought so," Pudding said. "But don't his friends wonder about the doors when they come to visit?"

"Oh, they've asked about them all right. Master just tells them the truth, that he has an Elf living here."

"What do they say?"

"They think Master is a little fluffy in the upstairs. You know, cuckoo. I've seen them laugh at him behind his back. He doesn't have as many friends coming over as he used to."

"Couldn't he show them Old Toaster?" Pudding asked.

"That's a silly question. You should know better. Conversations with someone who would sound to them like a mouse? No, it wouldn't work. They'd think he was fluffier than ever. Anyway, Master doesn't care. He tells Old Toaster that he and I are all the friends he needs."

Thor's eyes became distant and dreamy. "We have great times in the library, the three of us."

"What . . . what do the three of you do?"

"Talk. At least Old Toaster and Master do. Most of the conversation is over my head, so I have to admit I sleep through a great deal."

"What do they talk about?" Pudding asked wistfully.

"History mostly. Elf history. Furken history especially." Thor scratched his ear thoughtfully. His leg thump-thumped on the floor. "Funny I never caught all that about vanishing. I must have slept right through it."

For a long time, Pudding just sat and stared at the floor. A small brass clock on the kitchen table drummed a tiny beat through the silent room. "Brave, brave, not so brave," it seemed to say. A night bug skittered across the moonlit linoleum and disappeared under the stove. "Exactly like us!" Pudding said to himself, and threw himself down on the floor.

"What is it? What's wrong?" Thor asked anxiously.

"I want to be friends with Noah, too!" Pudding said angrily. "I want to have great times in the library and talk about brave deeds. I *know* about Furkens *now*. I want to know about Furkens *then*! Why can't I come to the library, too?"

"I wish I could help," Thor said gently. "But I can't do anything about Old Toaster. He's set on keeping Noah to himself." Thor paused a moment. "Look," he said, "I have an idea. Why don't I take you on a tour of the house before you go back down? Wouldn't you like that?"

"I can't!" Pudding said miserably. "I shouldn't even be in the kitchen."

"Horsefeathers!" said Thor. "Look, climb aboard my neck. I'll sit very still. You can hang onto my collar, and we'll take a jaunt around the house."

"Well . . ."

"Oh, come on!" said Thor.

Pudding drew a deep breath and climbed on Thor's neck. A moment later he felt the exciting motion of the great dog tilting, rising, and padding out of the kitchen.

It was the most wonderful experience Pudding had ever had in his life, loping along, clinging to Thor's neck. He felt as if he were a Furken of old, riding on his Elf charger to perform great deeds of glory. It didn't seem to matter that all they were doing was riding out of a kitchen, through a dining room, into a library, and finally up plain, ordinary stairs to a plain, ordinary upstairs hall.

"Faster, Thor!" Pudding cried. "Can't you go faster?"

"What for?" Thor said, laughing.

"I want to hear the wind whistle in my ears!"

"If I go any faster in the house, I'll ram into a door and kill us both," said Thor. "One day I'll take you for a ride in the garden. *Then* we'll make the wind whistle in your ears!"

"Couldn't I at least climb onto the bannister and slide down it?" Pudding asked when they were ready to return downstairs.

"Do you think you should?" Thor said.

"I don't know why not. Please let me!" Pudding pleaded.

"Oh, all right!" Thor laughed and edged up to the bannister.

Pudding swung himself over to it from Thor's neck, swallowed hard, and then let himself start sliding downward. It was only then that he realized there was no way to stop himself at the bottom! The waxed bannister was slippery as melted butter. Pudding slid faster and faster. "Thor, help!" he cried.

Then he flew out into space. He was holding onto nothing, and nothing was all around. Everything seemed to spin around him.

Suddenly he was caught in something soft and warm. The soft warm thing closed over him, and he lay inside it in the blackness, panting with fear. A moment later, the blackness parted, like a stage curtain, and moonlight poured over him.

"Well, what have we here?" said Noah Ebenezer Bender, peering down into his hand.

SIX

Worse and Worse

"I . . . I . . . I . . ." Pudding stammered. Words froze in his throat like little slivers of ice.

"Yes?" Noah's voice was stern, though Pudding had the distinct feeling that his eyes were twinkling.

"I'm Pudding!"

"So I suspected," said Noah. He rubbed his chin and looked thoughtfully down at the hand that held Pudding. "Well, I see Toaster was right. You simply couldn't be trusted."

"I didn't mean to! I didn't mean to come into the kitchen!" Pudding cried desperately.

"Ah, but you *did*! Now the question remains, what are we going to do about it, eh? What do you suggest, Toaster?"

Pudding looked down at the floor, and his heart nearly stopped beating. Standing on the first step of the stairway, arms crossed, and staring back at him balefully, was Old Toaster!

"Send them both packing!" snorted the old Furken.

"Now, Toaster," said Noah, "let's be reasonable."

"Well," returned Old Toaster huffily, "you asked what I suggested."

"Oh please!" Pudding blurted out. "If . . . if you must send someone away, send *me*! It wasn't Muddle's fault. He warned me and warned me, and I promised. Please don't send *him*!"

Noah smiled down on Pudding. His eyes were warm and kind as he set Pudding gently on the floor. "There now, nobody is sending anyone anywhere. We must simply talk this over. Thor!" he exclaimed suddenly. "where are you going?"

As they were talking, Thor had loped down the stairs and was now slinking into the kitchen, his tail tucked tightly downward. In reply to Noah's question, he stopped and uttered a guilty whine.

"I have a strong feeling, Toaster," Noah said, "that our dog friend had an important hand in all of this. Why don't you have a talk with him right now. And implore him to be totally honest," he added, raising an eyebrow.

Old Toaster strode purposefully toward Thor and ordered him to drop to the floor. A low-voiced conversation then took place between them, with Thor snuffling and grunting and thumping his tail on the floor, and Old Toaster looking crosser and crosser as he spoke. Finally, in what looked like a supreme effort to show how sorry he was. Thor rolled over on his back with his paws raised toward the ceiling and his tail smacking the floor. He looked so silly that even Pudding felt like laughing, but Old Toaster stomped back to the stairs, frowning.

"Well," said Noah, "was I right?"

"As usual!" groused Old Toaster. "But don't feel so pleased with yourself. It's your fault, you know, filling the dog's head with all that legal nonsense . . . didn't open the door, only stepped through it. Clear case of open and shut, indeed! Hmmmmph!" Lips tight with disapproval, Old Toaster thrust his chin down into his striped muffler.

"I didn't know I'd done any such thing. If I have, and it's turned out badly, then I'm sorry indeed," said Noah. "But, begging your pardon, Toaster, may we . . . er . . . consider *this* case closed?"

Thor's tail thumped hopefully on the floor.

"Oh, I suppose so," Old Toaster grumped at last. "Nothing to be done about it now."

"Splendid!" said Noah, stifling a yawn. "Now it's way past my bedtime and I—"

"Mr. Noah!" The words exploded from Pudding like a cork from a soda bottle.

"Yes?"

"Mr. Noah . . ." Pudding couldn't put into words the blinding, unbelievably mind-spinning thought that had popped into his head.

"It's all right, Pudding, you can tell me," Noah prompted him gently.

"Could I come to the library sometimes when you and Old Toaster talk about Furken history? I'll sit very quietly in a corner and not say a word. I'll only listen. Oh, please won't you let me!"

"I don't see why you shouldn't," Noah replied, smiling. "Do you, Toaster?"

Old Toaster gave an anguished sigh. "Yes, but why mention it. You'll only twist my poor brains until I say it's all right anyway. Might just as well save us both the trouble."

"I thought you'd see it that way!" Noah exclaimed. "And I suppose you wouldn't mind including your friend, Muddle, eh, Pudding?"

"Oh yes, please!" Pudding breathed.

"Worse and worse!" said Old Toaster, lifting his eyes toward the ceiling and groaning.

"Well then," said Noah, "I do believe it's all settled. And now, if you gentlemen will excuse me . . ."

He turned toward the stairs, but just as he started up them, he turned and gave Pudding a solemn, slow wink, as if to say that somehow he had known this would happen and had wanted it all along.

SEVEN

A Dance for Noah

Pudding climbed up the ladder leading to the chair seat, shoved his feet into the tiny pair of red leather slippers waiting there for him, and threw himself comfortably back against the chair arm. He wiggled his toes appreciatively, liking the way they popped in and out of the holes at the end of the slippers.

The only sounds in the library were the fire crackling and Thor snuffling in his sleep under Noah's legs.

Pudding had his own green leather chair now, studded with bright brass hobnails. He had found it waiting for him soon after he and Muddle had started coming to the library, along with the red leather slippers, and his own tiny silver drinking mug like Old Toaster's. From it he drank a clear amber liquid that tasted of roasted nuts, wild strawberries, and wood violets. It was concocted by

Noah from an ancient Elf recipe and tasted delicious.

The table before his chair, littered with papers and books, held a tray filled with dishes of crackers, creamy golden cheese, buttered muffins, and a cut-glass bowl of shimmering strawberry preserves. It was just as Thor said: Noah's between-the-meals were splendid.

Muddle, also wearing toeless red leather slippers, and a striped muffler as well, shared Old Toaster's chair, leaning against the opposite arm. His head was nodding, and his eyes drifting shut. Suddenly, he issued a loud, shuddering snore. Old Toaster quickly jumped up, crossed the chair, and dug him soundly in the ribs.

"Uh! Oh! What? Oh yes!" said Muddle. He straightened up against the chair, widened his eyes to look as if he were paying strict attention, but somehow managing to look as if he were still fast asleep. Muddle might have had his own chair, but Old Toaster had suggested they sit together so that he could keep Muddle quiet. Even Muddle agreed that this was a very good plan.

A thinking silence fell in the room once again. The fire continued to crackle. Thor whined in his sleep.

Noah shifted one foot over the other on the oak table. "Now, Toaster, on the matter of the Century of the Dragon Song we were discussing, I still insist that Flinting was the one who destroyed the Gorgondrock. Sliced his poisoned wings to ribbons, if I'm not mistaken. It left him harmless as a jellyfish on the hot sand."

"I'll agr-r-ree on the fact," said Old Toaster, "that it *was* Flinting who did in the Gor-r-r-gondr-r-rock, though

I'll wager he had a bit of help from the Bat Queen and her hirelings. Not, mind you, that she was ever a friend of Flinting's, but she was less a friend of the Gorgondrock! Still, Noah, I must continue to disagree with you on the time that it happened. I'd say it was closer to the Age of the Moon Slice."

"You could be right there, my good friend," replied Noah, "though I'm not saying definitely that you are, you understand, until I've had the chance to look into it thoroughly. But speaking of Moon Slice, that reminds me of the siege of Black Storming by the Sea. Do you remember . . ."

Pudding's mind began to drift. Dragon Song, Moon Slice, and Lost Sun! The cities of Black Storming and Wind Dark! Gorgondrock, Wolderblast, and Murking, the Enemies! And the great heroes: Flinting, Boldlock, and Fearnaught, Steelshine, Burnbold, and Kingsword! These were the words he had been hearing now for weeks. They were bold, brave names, and they told of the time in history when Furkens were still a fearless breed of Elves. Pudding said them over and over again to himself just to hear the sound. He dreamed of them at night.

"Why so glum, young man?" Noah asked. "Your mind has been lost to us ever since you came in this evening."

Pudding sighed. "I want to know why I wasn't born long ago when Furkens were proper Elves. They weren't afraid of anything then. I wish I were something besides a Furken boy named *Pudding*!"

Thor twisted his head restlessly in his sleep as if he had heard this.

"Well," Old Toaster said, stretching contentedly in his chair, "if you must be something else, then I say you should be a Furken philosopher as I am. In my old age, I enjoy talking of brave deeds, not doing them. If someone in the ancient past has done them, I say hurrah for them! As for me, I'm perfectly happy to read about it in books."

"I'm not!" said Pudding. "Noah, do you think Furkens were brave because they could vanish, or could they vanish because they were brave?"

Noah rubbed his chin thoughtfully. "That's a hard question to answer, Pudding. But knowing their history as I do, I'd have to say that I believe they could vanish because they were brave."

"But how can I be brave if I'm not?" asked Pudding, frowning.

"That's another hard question. I really can't answer it. Perhaps it has something to do with remembering things long forgotten, or simply wanting, or believing. Or perhaps all three."

"Would a sword make me brave?" Pudding asked.

"A sword?" Noah smiled. "Now where did you get an idea like that?"

"I don't know. I just did," Pudding replied. "But would you make me one, Noah?"

For a long time, Noah sat staring into the fire. "We'll see," he said at last softly. Then he dropped his feet off the table. "Now Toaster, how about a little muffin and cheese, eh?"

"I couldn't possibly, Noah," replied Old Toaster, with a quick sideways glance at Muddle and Pudding. "It's not Elf food, as you well know!"

"Yes, I do know indeed, but here, have a little anyway." Noah continued spreading cheese and part of a plump strawberry on a small piece of muffin. "It won't hurt just this once."

"Well, just this once," said Old Toaster, rolling his eyes as if the whole idea was slightly painful to him. "And . . . and you might fix a little for Pudding and Muddle, too, while you're at it."

Pudding looked across at Muddle, who had awakened at the very first mention of something to eat, but neither of them so much as started to smile. If Old Toaster wanted to carry on the game, as he had on all the evenings before this one, it was perfectly all right with them. It didn't hurt anyone a bit!

"And now that everyone is refreshed," said Noah, "I would like to say that I think it's high time you danced for me!"

"Dance?" said Old Toaster. He looked as if he were going to plummet off his chair.

"Yes, *dance*," said Noah firmly. "Muddle and Pudding dance, I know, and there's no reason at all why you shouldn't join them."

"I've forgotten how," Old Toaster grumbled.

"Nonsense! No one ever forgets how to dance," retorted Noah.

"My gout!" said Old Toaster, grabbing his toe and looking up at Noah as pitifully as he knew how.

"You old fraud!" said Noah, grinning. "You've never had a day of gout in your life. Come along now, I'll move the table to one side, and the three of you shall dance for me by the fireside." Then, as he was pulling the table away from the hearth, he threw out the words carelessly, "It will be a farewell gift to me!"

"Farewell gift!" exclaimed Old Toaster.

"Farewell gift!" echoed Muddle and Pudding in stunned voices.

"Please explain yourself, Noah!" said Old Toaster sternly.

Noah laughed. "It's nothing to be upset about. I'm not leaving for a few days and then will only be gone a fortnight. Thor will have to go to the kennel while I'm away, but the rest of you can carry on as always. I'm sorry there won't be a fire in the fireplace, but there's no reason why you can't continue to meet in the library."

"It won't be the same, Noah," said Pudding glumly.

"Perhaps not, Pudding," Noah replied. "But it won't be forever either. Now, come along, the three of you dance for me. Dance for me every night until I leave, and while I'm away, too. It will make the time pass quickly, and before any of us know it, I'll be home again!"

EIGHT

Swords

"It's been splendid, seeing you and Muddle and Old Toaster dance on the hearth for Master," Thor said to Pudding as they strolled in the garden three nights later. "Hearing the snap and crackle of the fire and seeing the shadows dancing along with you on the walls. Toaster still dances as if he needed to be oiled, but I've never seen Master have a better time than when he's watching the three of you."

"I'm glad," Pudding said. "Thor, will he really only be gone two weeks?" he asked anxiously.

"That's what he says. It will be a long two weeks for me!" Thor said, groaning.

"It will be for me, too," Pudding told him.

"But at least you won't be cooped up in a cage. I wish Master could take me with him, though I know he can't.

He's going to see his cousins, and they don't like me very well. I don't think they like Master, either. They think he's a little fluffy like everyone else. I wouldn't be surprised if they're not just waiting for the chance to tuck him away someplace." Thump! Thump! Thump! Thor's tail drummed angrily on the packed dirt.

"Why is he going then?" asked Pudding.

"It's some family business that has to be sorted out, he says. I wish he didn't have to go. I'm going to hate it!"

"I'm sorry, Thor," Pudding said. And he really was. The thought of this great dog in a place just big enough to turn around, surrounded by wire bars, brought tears to his eyes. To be in a cage would be a terrible thing for anyone. Pudding could hardly imagine how it would feel.

Silence fell over them.

"Thor . . ." Pudding's voice was hesitant, "have you heard Noah mention anything about my sword?"

"Not in my presence," Thor said.

"Not in mine either," said Pudding. "Not one word! Now he's going away."

"Why don't you bring the subject up again?" Thor looked at Pudding with warm, understanding eyes.

But Pudding squirmed uncomfortably. "I . . . I just couldn't, Thor."

"Well, perhaps he'll have it for you when he comes back."

"I don't think so," Pudding said. "I think he's forgotten all about it, or . . . or doesn't want me to have one."

"Look," Thor said suddenly, "why don't you climb

up on my neck, and we'll go for a ride. It will take our minds off our troubles."

Pudding didn't hesitate a minute. "All right!" he said. He had permission to take rides on Thor's neck as long as he didn't try anything dangerous. He loved riding Thor anytime Thor was willing to take him. Thor lowered his neck, and Pudding clambered on.

It was beautiful in the garden. Even though Noah continued to light a fire for them every night in the library, spring had really arrived. The apple tree was drifting in its own pale blossoms. A willow tree at the end of the garden had long since begun to show green. The air was filled with the pungent smell of moss.

Pudding dug his heels into Thor's neck. He knew it would feel like no more than two falling acorns to Thor, but the dog knew what he wanted. It was a game they played. Thor reared back with a snort, threw his head up, and charged off down the path.

"Take me to the crabapple tree!" Pudding commanded.

"What are you going to do there?" Thor asked.

"You'll see!"

"Now, put your paws on the trunk, and stretch as high as you can," Pudding told Thor when they had arrived at the tree. He looked up into the web of branches spreading out around them. Then he reached out and pulled a tiny twig from the tree.

"There!" Pudding announced triumphantly. "I have a sword!"

"What do you propose to do with it?" Thor asked.

Pudding swished the twig through the air. "I don't know. Just carry it around, I suppose."

"Well, you can carry it into the house then. Hold on, we're going back."

"Do we have to go in so soon?"

Thor's head tilted. "Listen! Do you hear that?"

"Thunder?"

"Yes," Thor said, "and I hate storms!"

Back in the house Pudding leaned over and whispered in Thor's ear. "Take me to the library and put me on the windowsill. I'll take care of this one for you!"

"What do you mean?" Thor asked anxiously.

"Wait, and I'll show you," Pudding said.

By the time Thor had let Pudding off onto the windowsill in the library, thunder was cracking the air around him. Brilliant flashes of lightning slashed their way into the room. Thor cringed in a corner, his nose under a chair. "I'm a coward when it comes to storms, and I make no bones about it," he told Pudding.

Pudding stood at the window, his tiny twig sword in his hand. A clap of thunder shook the room. He jabbed the twig at the window. "Take that!" he shouted.

With fierce determination, Pudding slashed the twig through the air. "Die, storm!" he roared at a flash of lightning. "You're just an empty bag of lights and noise. I'll finish you off once and for all! Take that and that!"

In a while, the sounds of the thunder began to

weaken. The flashes of lightning dimmed. Soon the only sound left in the room was the patter of raindrops on the windowsill.

"It's all right now, Thor," Pudding said. "I've killed the storm."

"I can still hear it a little," Thor said. His voice was quivering.

"Well, it may not be quite dead yet. But it's mortally wounded, and it's gone off to die."

"That was very brave, Pudding," Thor said. "Did your new sword make you brave?"

Pudding ran the twig through his fingers. "The storm would have died anyway, Thor. Killing it was only a game. The sword isn't a sword at all, it's only an apple twig, and I don't feel any braver than I did before."

Pudding cracked the twig over his leg and slowly let the pieces fall from his hand. Far below him, they lay on the library floor, looking small and broken and helpless.

In the morning, while Old Toaster, Muddle, and Pudding slept, Noah and Thor quietly left the house.

That evening, Old Toaster, Muddle, and Pudding went to the library just as they had promised Noah they would do. Without too much spirit, Pudding climbed the ladder to his chair. And there he found his surprise waiting for him!

"My sword! My sword!" he cried.

It was a real sword this time, not just a twig from a crabapple tree. Complete with its own little leather belt and sheath, it was made of shining steel, with a finely wrought hilt just big enough to fit Pudding's hand. Across the hilt was engraved a tiny shield. In one corner of the shield were three diamonds, each the size of half a mustard seed, and across the face of the shield was a Furken rampant.

"I'll always keep it with me," Pudding said. "It's the most beautiful thing I've ever seen. Did you know about it, Old Toaster?"

"I watched Noah making it!" Old Toaster said proudly.

Pudding rubbed his fingers over the three diamonds in the hilt. They felt pleasant to him, cold and hard. "Why did Noah put in diamonds?" he asked Old Toaster.

"To stand for something," Old Toaster replied. "For stars of remembering, wanting, and believing."

Pudding let his fingers run down the sword. It felt cold as the diamonds, but smooth as a piece of silk. Holding his breath, he slid it into the sheath that he had fastened to his waist. He expected to feel brave instantly. Still, when he felt nothing, he didn't worry about it. When the right time came, he was certain that the beautiful steel sword would make him just as brave as he would ever need to be.

NINE

Rented

Two weeks dragged slowly by.

For three evenings, Old Toaster, Muddle, and Pudding continued to meet in the library. Then they stopped. It seemed silly to sit and stare miserably at each other for an hour. Soon, Old Toaster and Muddle stopped going into the house at all. Old Toaster sometimes walked as far as the little stairs, looked up glumly, and then returned to the barrel. His skirt no longer swung briskly back and forth. It hung limply to his knees.

Pudding went into the house, though he went by himself. Sometimes he climbed up onto his chair in the library just to sit. Other times he sat by the brown bowl on the kitchen floor, tracing with a finger the white letters that spelled the word "DOG." He missed Thor terribly. But most of the time he wandered aimlessly from room to empty room, kicking hair-width tracks in the dust.

One day shortly before Noah and Thor were to return, Pudding made a broom of dried grass stalks and climbed into Thor's bowl. Clouds of dust rose up from it as he swept. Not until he was satisfied that he could see his face reflected in the bowl once again did he climb back out.

But when the two weeks had ended, Thor and Noah did not return. They did not return the next day, or the day after that. The dust settled in Thor's bowl once more.

"What if he never comes back?" Muddle asked Old Toaster. His eyes darted anxiously around the firethorn bush where they were sitting and holding a conference.

"He'll come back!" Pudding cried. "He wouldn't *not* come back without telling us, would he, Old Toaster?"

"Never-r-r!" said Old Toaster.

But Muddle's face turned green as a spring onion. "What if the rats come? Will we have to move?"

"They haven't come yet, Muddle," Pudding said. He sucked thoughtfully on a stalk of sourgrass. "Why do we have to do anything? Why can't we just go on waiting until Noah and Thor come home?"

"Pudding's right," Old Toaster said. "Why do anything?"

Why indeed? they all agreed at last, and went on waiting.

But Old Toaster seemed to grow older, more bent and more gray. He refused to dance anymore. Finally, Muddle and Pudding stopped dancing, too. Muddle wrapped his muffler about his throat and took to his bed. Pudding spent most of his time lying on his back under the crabapple tree, rubbing a finger up and down the cold steel of his sword, staring at the sky.

In the house, the dust fell and fell.

Pudding woke suddenly from a dream in which he was walking through a dark, silent forest. It seemed that the sharp snap of a twig had awakened him. He looked around in a daze and was surprised to find that he was in the library. Then he remembered that he had come into the house about midday. He had climbed onto his chair, where he must have fallen asleep on a spot of leather warmed by the sun. The sharp snap he had heard was the click of a door closing.

Voices drifted into the library from the hall, but they were the voices of a strange man and woman. The man's voice wasn't Noah's. And there was no friendly sound of Thor's paws pad-padding across the floor.

Quickly, Pudding leaped down the ladder and raced across the library floor to a small skirted chair that sat in a corner. There he dove under the skirt and lay panting, waiting to hear what the voices would say.

They faded and finally disappeared as the two people went upstairs. Then they came back down, and Pudding heard them going into the dining room and kitchen. Words floated in to him, but they were senseless words. They had no real meaning. "Oh yes, of course, the coat closet." "Old fashioned." "Expect that." "Splendid size, nevertheless." "But will it do?" The last words were accompanied by a deep sigh.

At last the voices arrived in the library. Pudding peeked out from under the chair skirt to see what he could tell from the faces that went with them. The woman's face wore the curiously blank expression of a shopper who has said, "Just looking, thanks," when asked if she would like help.

The man's face was smiling, but worried. "There's a basement, too, you know," he said. "Are you certain you wouldn't like to see it?"

"It won't be necessary," the woman replied. "You say you're certain he's not coming back?"

"Not for the time you'll be wanting the house. It really isn't likely that he'll be back at all."

"Oh?" questioned the woman.

The man lowered his voice as if he were talking in a sick room in front of the patient. "He became ill when he was visiting relatives. They have him in a home now."

"He isn't expected to get well?" the woman asked.

The man shrugged. "He's a little"—his voice dropped even lower—"*you* know, *off*."

"Off?"

"He claims he has an Elf living with him!" The man began to chuckle as if somewhere, hidden in what he'd said, was a huge joke. "I suppose that explains the little doors."

"Why yes, I suppose it does," the woman said doubtfully. Then her eyebrows flew up her forehead. "There's nothing else peculiar about the house, is there?"

"Oh no!" the man assured her.

But the woman looked at him sideways. "Of course, the rent *is* high."

"I'm sure that can be taken care of," the man said quickly.

The woman's face began to wear a satisfied expression, as if perhaps she weren't "just looking" after all.

"It's a pity," she said. "About the old man, I mean. The house will be sold in time, no doubt."

"No doubt," the man said blankly.

They started out of the room. "By the way, I forgot to mention," the woman said, "it won't be just my husband and myself in the house. We have my nine-year-old nephew with us. I don't suppose there's any objection to a boy in the house, is there?"

"Oh, absolutely not!" the man said, smiling broadly. "No objection at all!"

TEN

Freddy

"A Human *boy!*" Old Toaster screamed, and promptly collapsed onto the floor.

"What's so terrible about a Human boy?" Pudding asked.

Old Toaster raised himself up weakly on one arm. "They're cur-r-r-rious," he said grimly. "They don't let things alone. They poke and they explore. They investigate . . . and they *discover!*" He groaned and collapsed again.

Muddle looked as if he might collapse right on top of Old Toaster. "Wha . . . wha . . . wha . . . what are we going to do? Will we have to leave the house now?"

"Never-r-r!" said Old Toaster. He struggled to his feet and stood stiff as a tree stump with his chin high in the air. "If you want to go, you have my blessing. But I'm going to stay here and wait for Noah!"

Muddle and Pudding exchanged long, searching looks. Then Muddle turned to Old Toaster. "So will we!" he said.

"I'm glad to hear it," Old Toaster returned. Then, to hide his embarrassment, he began marching up and down in front of them, his hands behind his back, studying the ground. "Of course, we'll have to leave the barrel. We'd have to do that anyway," he added, as if it needed to be explained, "boy or no boy."

"Wha . . . wha . . . wha . . . where will we go?" Muddle asked. His two chins were quivering, though he was trying hard to control his voice.

"We could move in behind the boxes in the corner," Pudding said eagerly. "The ones where Noah stores his old law books."

"Yes!" Muddle chimed in. "It will be just like Pudding's and my old home, where we lived behind the orange crate."

"Not the same thing at all," Old Toaster said. "These boxes might be taken away. If they're not, the boy will move them." He shuddered. "Boys move everything! But wait a moment, let me think."

As Muddle and Pudding watched him anxiously, he continued marching in front of them. His skirt swished over his knees in a businesslike manner.

"There's a place," he muttered, almost more to himself than anyone else. "There's a place I found once. It was . . . it was . . . yes, it was *there!*" Old Toaster pointed a stiff finger to a place where the wall joined the ceiling. "Up there, I found a small crack once when I first settled in the basement. Noah told me then that I should always remember it 'just in case,' as he said, but I didn't. Until now!"

"What does a crack have to do with anything?" asked Muddle, looking totally confused.

"It has to do with what's behind it!" replied Old Toaster. "It won't be so pleasant or so comfortable as the barrel, but it would be a place to live . . . and hide! It can't be taken away, and the boy can't move it."

"Behind a wall!" Muddle cried. His eyes were shot through with horror. "Like *mice!*"

"We can't worry about *how* we live," Old Toaster said grimly. "What we have to worry about is whether we live at all, with a nine-year-old Human boy in the house!"

Nobody needed to announce a few days later that the boy, with his aunt and uncle, had come to live in the house. He was called Freddy.

His heavy footsteps crashed through the house, pounding up the stairs only to come pounding right back down again. He made strange, wild, gurgling animal sounds in his throat to accompany himself wherever he went. He seemed to do everything with the simple purpose in mind of making as big a racket as possible. There was one good thing about this, Old Toaster remarked. You could always tell where he was at any moment of the day. But that was the only good thing.

Freddy, just as Old Toaster had predicted, was curious. The racket moved from room to room in a regular pattern as if he was, indeed, exploring. And it was less than half an hour after he arrived that he came thumping down into the basement.

Pudding lay on his stomach, just inside the crack on the ledge, watching the solid, stocky figure with the clumping brown oxford shoes move noisily around the room.

Everything interested Freddy, even the cracks in the cement floor, which he stooped to examine. But the things that aroused his interest most were the two miniature stairways. He must have found the little door into the kitchen earlier and had it explained to him, because he paid no attention to it. The other door, the one to the tunnel, was a new discovery. But the door was way over his head near the roof of the basement, much too high for him to reach. His bright blue eyes darted swiftly around the basement, and a moment later he was dragging across the floor a wooden folding ladder he had seen lying on its side under the big stairs. It made a terrible scraping sound on the floor, but Freddy seemed to like this. He even moved the ladder back and forth a few times just to repeat the noise.

Once the ladder had been set up, he climbed it

quickly. The ladder was just tall enough so that by climbing as high as he dared, his eyes reached the ledge. He raised one hand and began carefully to open and close the little door.

"What if he nails it shut?" Pudding wondered, shuddering. They had laid up a supply of food in their hiding place, but it couldn't last forever. Nor could the walnut shells full of water they had painstakingly, and dangerously, carried across the ledge to the crack in the ceiling. If the door to the tunnel was sealed, they would starve to death, or die of thirst.

But Freddy only played on the ladder for a while, then something caught his eye on the floor of the basement. He closed the little door and bump-bump-bumped down the ladder. He stumped across the floor excitedly, and a moment later Pudding found himself looking almost directly down on Freddy's thick, tumbling, sandy hair as he knelt on the ground before the barrel, humming a tuneless little tune and studying it carefully.

"It's the man's Elf house!" Freddy breathed. "It's where he thought he had an Elf living." He stood up and began doing a funny little jig step, as if the excitement of his find was too much for him. He dropped back down to his knees and began poking his fingers into the doors and windows, peering through with one eye, and finally going down on his stomach to look in Old Toaster's den.

"A fireplace!" he exclaimed. "And furniture!"

It didn't take him long to discover that he could lift

off the top of the barrel and look down into Muddle and Pudding's attic apartment. Then he began to pull out the furniture.

Old Toaster had finally decided that they must leave almost everything in the barrel. It had turned out to be too difficult and dangerous even to move something as small as chairs across the ledge. In the end, all they had taken with them were acorn cups, the walnut shell bowls, and enough oak leaves for their beds. So there was a great deal left in the barrel for Freddy to pull out.

He examined curiously the little dry sinks, the tables and chairs, and the cupboards, opening with the greatest interest the tiny doors and drawers. From where Pudding lay, everything looked terribly small and fragile in Freddy's thick, clumsy hands.

Squatting before the barrel, intent on his work, Freddy had become very, very quiet. He was no longer making the strange noises in his throat, or even humming the tuneless little tune.

"He really can be quiet, when he wants to be!" Pudding thought, and wasn't certain whether he liked the idea or not.

Then, as if he had been chained by his deep thoughts and suddenly let loose, Freddy jumped up, and with a howl of delight, went pounding across the basement to the stairs. He held Old Toaster's cupboard in one hand and waved it wildly in the air.

"Aunt Clara! Aunt Clara!" he screamed, and went

clumping up the stairs two at a time. Pudding could hear the brown oxfords drum across the kitchen linoleum as Freddy went in search of his aunt to announce his discovery.

Pudding turned around to make his own trembling report to Old Toaster and Muddle, cowering in the darkness behind him.

Freddy came to the basement to play with the barrel nearly every day. Sometimes the games he played were his usual noisy ones, racing small cars around the barrel, marching plastic soldiers in and out of it, or shoving small stuffed animals through the doors where they would stand and make their loud animal noises. But most of the time he was very quiet when he played with the barrel, humming his tuneless little tune, or being absolutely silent.

Pudding liked watching Freddy play. He almost always crept up to the crack whenever he heard the heavy oxfords clumping down the stairs. Freddy seemed to have finished with exploring and be quite content with what he had found. He never looked up from his play. Sometimes Pudding crept almost all the way through the crack and peered down over the ledge. Old Toaster and Muddle even stopped warning him to be careful. He felt quite safe now.

Late one afternoon, when Old Toaster and Muddle

were still fast asleep, Pudding heard the familiar pound-pound-pound coming down the stairs. This was followed by the sound of the ladder scraping across the floor. But there was no thump-thump-thump of Freddy's feet going up the ladder. This made Pudding curious.

He slipped quietly out from under his covers, dropped silently to his stomach, and inched out toward the crack. There was no sign of Freddy anywhere, not by the barrel, not in any corner, and not even standing on the ladder by the little door that led into the tunnel. Nor was there any sign of the ladder. Freddy and his ladder had vanished!

Pudding slid out a little further, and just as he did, the ten fingers of two hands crept over the ledge, and between them rose a head of sandy hair, and two terrifyingly bright blue eyes. Long lashes stood out from the lids like centipede legs. Slowly they dropped over the eyes and rose again. Beyond that, Freddy was motionless. Silently, he and Pudding stared at one another.

Suddenly, Pudding recovered from the shock and surprise of finding Freddy less than two inches away from him. He slithered back through the crack in the ceiling, and lay with his heart pounding. Freddy's breath began to come from his throat in a hoarse whisper. Pudding felt the warm, moist air rolling over him. It smelled of cinnamon.

One blue eye appeared briefly at the opening. Then it moved away, and a chubby finger pushed its way in and began waving around like a minature giraffe's neck. In a moment, it went away, too. The eye appeared again.

"Come back, mouse!" Freddy said. "Come where I can see you."

Pudding lay perfectly still, breathing in tiny half breaths of air.

"Never mind then," Freddy said softly. "I know you're in there. I'll see you again. Good-bye, mouse!"

The eye disappeared from the crack. The footsteps went thump-thump-thump down the ladder. Then there was the surprising sound of the ladder being scraped back across the basement floor. Freddy rarely put anything away. What he moved in the basement, he always left just where he had finished playing with it. But Pudding heard him panting with the effort of shoving the ladder back under the steps where it was kept.

In horror, he waited for Freddy to run screaming up to the kitchen for his Aunt Clara, to tell her about his new discovery. But all Freddy did after he put the ladder away was to walk softly up the steps. He hardly made any sound at all.

❧

The next afternoon, Pudding peeked through the crack and saw Aunt Clara descending the basement stairs in huge green fuzzy slippers that looked like a pair of caterpillars. She looked so sternly determined that he was certain she was coming to get them. But apparently she was not. She began to unpack a battered black footlocker. Soon the floor was littered with sweaters and blankets, and the basement smelled of mothballs. Shortly afterwards, Freddy thumped down the stairs.

He stood by his aunt for a few moments, staring first into the trunk and then at her interesting slippers. She didn't pay any attention to him, so he picked up a blanket from the floor and unfolded it. Mothballs rolled across the floor.

"Freddy, be careful," she said absently.

Freddy half folded the blanket and dropped it back on the floor.

"Aunt Clara?"

"Hmmmm?"

"I want to know more about the man who lived here and the Elf," Freddy said.

"I told you we're not going to talk about him anymore!" Aunt Clara replied firmly.

"But why?" insisted Freddy.

Aunt Clara gave a weary sigh. "Because it's a silly subject. The man is sick, and there's no such thing as an Elf. I really don't want to hear about it again."

"Why do you let me play with the barrel then?" Freddy continued stubbornly.

"Because it was left here with the furniture, and it makes a nice toy. But if you're going to keep bothering me about it, I won't let you play with it anymore." Aunt

Clara's lips pressed firmly together with this warning.

"Well"—Freddy looked at Aunt Clara sideways—"I think *I* know what the Elf was!"

"Oh, you do know, do you? And what do you think it was?"

"I think the man had a trained mouse to live in the barrel and go through all the little doors. It wasn't an Elf he had, but a mouse!"

"Don't be silly, Freddy. No one could train a mouse to do all those things. You're letting your imagination run away with you again."

Freddy scowled. "Well, I . . . I . . ." He hesitated, looking up at the ceiling. ". . . I *still* think it was a mouse!"

Suddenly, Aunt Clara slammed down the lid of the foot locker and leaped up onto it. One green fuzzy caterpillar slipper went sailing across the basement floor. "You didn't *see* a mouse, did you?" she shrieked. "You haven't found a mouse anywhere? You know how I feel about mice!"

Freddy looked down at the floor and scuffed his foot back and forth. When he looked up, his face was blank. "No," he said. "I never saw one."

"You're quite certain?"

"Yes," said Freddy.

ELEVEN

Trapped

It was late afternoon again when Pudding slid through the crack onto the ledge. His sword was in the sheath by his side. He'd been listening for a long time and was certain that Freddy wasn't around. The only sounds in the basement were those that sifted down through the floorboards of the remote house above it.

Pudding had been warned sternly by Old Toaster never to go out on the ledge again except when they all went together in the dead of night to gather food in the garden.

"He'll be watching every minute," this expert on Human boys said. "You can mar-r-rk my wor-r-rds. He'll be watching, more than ever before!"

"But he didn't tell his Aunt Clara about me," Pudding said. "Nobody's put out a mousetrap."

"Mousetrap, hmmmmph!" snorted Old Toaster. "Human boys don't take stock in anything as honest as a mousetrap. To them it's the sport that matters. They like to see how long they can keep things going in boxes and cages. He's got one lying about. You can be cer-r-rtain of that!"

But that was all days ago now. Freddy seemed to have forgotten all about finding a mouse. He never pulled the ladder up to the wall, not any wall. He was noisy when he played by the barrel. He never crept around being secretive, as if he might be trying to catch something.

The basement looked quiet and peaceful in the afternoon sun. It was a long time since Pudding had seen the sunlight. He pulled his sword from its sheath and held it out over the ledge to see if he could catch a gleam of light on the metal. The sun caught as well the three diamonds and, for a moment, blinded him. Just then he heard Freddy's feet pounding through the house. The sword slipped from his fingers and went down, down, down, striking the cement below with a little plink. It lay there, looking back at him like a tiny, glittering pin.

By now, Freddy's feet had pounded into the kitchen, and there was nothing Pudding could do but slide back through the crack into darkness and safety. His sword, the beautiful sword that Noah had made for him, lay below him, miles and miles below, it seemed, on the cold, hard, cement floor.

Pudding couldn't very well tell Old Toaster what

had happened. He couldn't tell Muddle either. It wouldn't help him if he did. They considered it much too dangerous to go down the little steps at any time, for any reason. Neither of them had ventured down since they had moved out of the barrel, nor had they let Pudding go. If he was going to get his sword back at all, he knew he would have to do it without anyone knowing it, and he would have to do it alone.

Pudding lay stiffly in his bed that night, waiting for everyone to drop off to sleep. His insides felt tight as a leather knot. It seemed hours before he finally heard Old Toaster grunting as he always did in his sleep and Muddle shaking the timbers with his snores. Pudding slid stealthily from under his covers and crept out the crack onto the ledge.

The furnace had been turned off for the summer and was still. The barrel and Freddy's mountain of toys lay like islands in the silent pools of moonlight. There was no comforting gleam of light from where the sword lay, but that didn't matter. Pudding knew exactly where it was, and once he was on the floor, he would have no trouble in finding it. He jumped up, shivering, and began the journey downward.

Moving swiftly over the ledge, down the steps, and across the basement floor, he arrived, panting heavily, at the place where he had dropped the sword. He fell to his knees to pick it up. But the sword was gone!

Wildly, Pudding crawled over the floor, his hands sweeping like little brooms before him to find it. Back and forth before the wall! Move away! Back and forth again! His hands and knees were smarting now from being scraped by the rough cement. Dry sobs caught in his throat as he felt the empty sheath by his side. But he knew now what had happened to his sword. Freddy had taken it! Sometime, amidst all the racket he was making, he must have crept up and made his discovery. Finders keepers! Now the sword belonged to *him*.

Where had he taken it? Could he have taken it to his room? Was it near him right this minute, hidden warmly in his pajama pocket as he slept? Where would a Human boy like this one keep such a treasure? Where had he kept his treasures in the past?

In the barrel! That's where Freddy stuffed everything these days. Hadn't they heard Aunt Clara muttering about the "rat's nest" whenever she came to the basement? Pudding strode grimly toward their old home. Freddy had stolen his sword, and he was going to get it back again!

On his way to the barrel, Pudding dug through mountains of Freddy's belongings that had once been in the barrel and now lay strewn around the floor. The sword could be buried under any of them. He pushed aside blocks, train tracks, and small metal cars. He dug under a small hill of bird feathers, an assortment of rocks, countless pencil stubs, a torn card of dried beetles with pins stuck through them, dozens of bent nails and jar caps, and the limp remains of two very large and at least fifteen small balloons. These last were very old and had a rubbery smell.

Directly outside the barrel, a worn plush rabbit lay on its stomach. Pudding pushed it aside, but all he found was a stale chocolate cupcake partially wrapped in a birthday party napkin, and next to it a torn woolen cap filled with sticky candy wrappers. There was no sword anywhere.

Now Pudding stood at the door of the barrel. A lump rose in his throat when he saw the moon shining off the little mushroom door handle and looked up at the familiar, brown-shuttered windows and the twisted chimney. He was trembling when he pushed open the door, remembering the very first time he had crossed the threshhold behind Old Toaster.

The sparkle of the diamonds caught his eye the moment he opened the door. Directly ahead of him, where the moonlight poured through a window, lay his sword! Pudding leaped through the doorway and snatched it up.

From behind him came the soft, slithering sound of metal sliding against smooth metal. It was followed by a small, firm click. Pudding whirled around.

There was no one behind him, but now a row of

thin, gleaming bars like metal teeth spread across the doorway. The moonlight shining through them made a shadowy network of lines on the floor. Pudding dropped the sword with a clatter and ran to the bars. He circled his hands around two of them and tried to shake them loose. They didn't even quiver. He looked from side to side, then over his head, and he saw with horror that the thin gleaming bars were all around him. This was a cage, Freddy's cage, and he was trapped in it!

In one corner of the cage, an exercise wheel wobbled slightly. In another hung two small bowls, one filled with water and the other with seeds. It was just such a Human boy's cage as Old Toaster had described.

Desperately, Pudding picked up his sword and began striking the bars of the cage with it. All they did was send back tiny musical notes to mock him.

"Old Toaster! Muddle!" Pudding cried, knowing that it was useless to call them. Muddle snored so loudly he could drown out a thunderstorm. He would sleep soundly until daylight and all through the day. Freddy would be down in the basement long before help could come.

Once Pudding had talked with Thor about cages. Then he could only imagine how terrible it would be. Now it seemed that he would find out all about it first-hand. He let his sword slip through his hand to the floor. Then, with a sob, he threw himself beside it and lay in the shadowy patches of moonlight to wait.

TWELVE

A Trained Mouse

The moon had faded, but it was still dark out when Pudding heard the slap-slap of bare feet coming down the basement steps. The feet padded across the floor. Suddenly a bright white light flashed through the door of the barrel into the cage, and Freddy gave a hoarse cry of pleasure.

Lying rigid beside his sword, Pudding listened to Freddy grunt as he lifted off the cover of the barrel, then the floor below it. A finger curled around a wire at the top of the cage, and Pudding felt it rise upward through the barrel at a dizzying rate.

Freddy shone his flashlight through the bars of the cage. He was breathing heavily with excitement.

"I knew you'd be there, mouse! You came after your

sword, didn't you? I was right. The old man's Elf *was* a trained mouse. It was you, and now you're mine! Now we're going upstairs to my room."

Clutching the cage tightly against his striped blue and white pajamas, Freddy crept on tiptoe up the two flights of stairs to his room. He closed the door softly and set the cage down on his bed with a thump. Inside the cage, the little wheel rattled, and water spilled from the water bowl. Pudding felt the water splashing on his feet, but he didn't move.

Freddy threw himself down on his stomach beside the cage, lay his chin down on the blanket, and stared through the bars.

"There, you blinked!" he said. "I didn't think you were dead. You're just pretending. But you don't have to. I'm not going to hurt you." He waited a moment. "Well then, *don't* move! You will soon. You can't lie there for-ever."

Suddenly, he rolled over on his back and kicked his feet in the air. "Mouse! Mouse! Mouse! Woweee! I have a trained mouse!" He jumped up from the bed and danced a silent jig around the room, hugging himself for joy. Then he flopped back down on the bed. A shower of water mixed with birdseed splashed over Pudding.

Freddy continued staring into the cage. In a while he began humming his familiar tuneless little tune. His face was so close to the cage that Pudding could count the freckles on his nose.

"You're a smart mouse," Freddy said. "I can tell by the way you look at me that you practically know what I'm saying to you. I'll bet the man taught you lots of tricks. I wonder how I can make you do some for me. Hmmm, hmmmmm, hm, hm, hm," he went on humming. "I know! We'll start with the easiest one. I'll bet you can run on the wheel. Even a *stupid* mouse could do that." Freddy took a pencil from the table by his bed and pushed it through the bars of the cage. The pencil nudged the wheel, and it began to spin.

Pudding had already decided he wouldn't speak to Freddy. What was the use? He'd only sound like a squeaking mouse. He'd also decided he wouldn't do any tricks. He wouldn't do anything but lie on the floor until Freddy gave up on him and let him go.

But supposing Freddy didn't let him go?

Why not do all the tricks Freddy wanted him to do, and let Freddy think he really was a trained mouse? Mightn't Freddy become very sure of Pudding then—and careless?

Besides this, Pudding didn't like the idea that any stupid mouse could do a trick that a descendant of brave Elves couldn't do. He jumped up and leaped onto the wheel. Freddy squealed with delight.

The trick wasn't nearly so easy as it looked. The wheel was already spinning fast, and Freddy kept nudging it with his pencil. Pudding's feet slipped through the wires. His knees and nose were scraped raw. In the end, the wheel threw him out onto the floor of the cage, where he landed in a sore and angry heap.

Freddy began to giggle. "I wish you could see yourself, mouse! You look pretty silly. I guess you're not as smart as I thought you were!"

Pudding stood up and thrust his sword furiously into its sheath. "Well, you're not so smart either! You must be pretty stupid if you think a mouse is *smart* enough to wear a sword, or come after it when he's lost it, or even live in a barrel. Trained mouse, toad tails! Your Aunt Clara is smarter than you are!"

Freddy stopped giggling. His eyes widened, and his long lashes swept down over his eyes in three unbelieving blinks.

"What was that you said?" he whispered.

"I said that you must be . . ." Pudding's voice trailed off into a kind of shocked silence.

For a long moment, neither one spoke.

"Can you . . . can you really understand what I'm saying?" Pudding asked.

Freddy nodded dumbly.

"You mean I don't just sound like a squeaking mouse to you?"

Freddy shook his head.

"Well, I'm not one," Pudding said. "It's what I was trying to tell you. I'm not a trained mouse. I'm a Furken."

"A what?" asked Freddy dimly.

"An Elf," said Pudding.

Color rushed back into Freddy's face. "There's no such thing as an Elf. You're lying!"

"Do you think there's such a thing as a talking mouse?" asked Pudding.

Freddy hesitated. "I've *read* about them."

"Have you ever met one?"

"No."

"You never will," said Pudding.

"Well, I don't think I'll *ever* meet an Elf either. Even if I did, how could I talk with him. Not everybody can talk with Elves, even in fairy tales. Why should I be able to talk with you?"

"I don't know," Pudding said truthfully. "Perhaps it's because you really believe in Elves."

Freddy's cheeks flushed a bright pink. "No, I don't!" he said defiantly.

"Noah believes in them. He could talk with us," Pudding said.

"Is Noah the old man who lived here?" Freddy asked.

Pudding nodded.

"Well, he was loony! Aunt Clara and Uncle Harry say so." Freddy chewed his lower lip nervously. "Nobody's ever going to say *I'm* loony!"

"Noah is not loony!" Pudding shouted furiously.

"He is too!" Freddy's face was turning an angry red. "He is too! And you *are* a mouse. You *look* just like a mouse!"

"I don't smell like one!" Pudding said haughtily. "If

you haven't already discovered it, I smell like a very high grade of warm apricot jam."

Freddy looked startled, as if he *had* already discovered it. He hesitated and then burst out, "So what! My Uncle Harry smells of spice after he shaves every morning. *He's* not an Elf. How you smell doesn't prove anything!"

The room was silent. Freddy sulked, picking at a corner of his blanket. Pudding gloomily rubbed his finger up and down his sword. At last he noticed that Freddy was staring into the cage once more. His face had returned to its natural color.

"That . . . that man, Noah," he began hesitantly, "was . . . was he the one who made the sword for you?"

Pudding sniffed and didn't reply. He still felt deeply injured.

"Please talk to me," Freddy pleaded. "My name is Freddy. Do you have a name?"

"Pudding," said Pudding grimly.

"Pudding?" Freddy giggled. "What kind of name is that?"

"You don't have to laugh. I didn't give it to myself," Pudding said.

"I'm sorry!" Freddy's eyes were eager now. "Did you and the man do things together? Did he carry you around in his pocket?"

Pudding drew himself up proudly. "We had lessons in the library!"

"Lessons?" Freddy wrinkled his nose. Then he

grinned. "Oh, you mean where he trained you to do tricks."

"We had lessons in *Elf history*," said Pudding, annoyed.

Freddy laughed. "Who ever heard of Elf history!"

"Noah did! He knew all about the Time of Red Burning, and Wind Dark, and the Age of the Moon Slice when the Gorgondrock roamed the Gloomy Places."

Freddy's eyes had begun to widen. "The Gorgondrock? Who was that?"

"He was one of the Evil Ones. There were lots of them. Noah taught me about all of them, and the brave Elf Heroes who slew them."

"Will you tell me about them?" Freddy asked.

"Why do you want to know Elf history if you don't believe in Elves?" Pudding said.

"I don't believe in lots of things, but I have to learn about them in school anyway," Freddy replied. "Please tell me!"

Pudding drew his sword from its sheath and nudged the wheel in the cage so that it began to spin slowly. "Will you take me out of the cage if I do?"

Freddy's hand moved toward the lock at the bottom of the cage door. Then suddenly it snapped back again. "I can't!" he said.

"Why not?"

"You'd run away!"

"I promise I won't," Pudding said. "You have the word of an Elf."

Freddy stared intently at his big toes. "I never said I believed you were an Elf. If you really were one, you could get out of the cage yourself. You could vanish, or something like that. I . . . I still think you're a mouse!"

"If I'm only a mouse," Pudding retorted, "I can't very well teach you about Elves, can I?"

Another angry silence filled the room. Finally, Freddy spoke. "I'm sorry about the cage. I . . . I can't help it. Please tell me about all those things you know!"

Something in Freddy's pleading voice made Pudding answer kindly. "Furkens used to be able to vanish. It's part of the history. If I tell it all to you and make you believe I really am an Elf, will you let me out of the cage then?"

For a long time, Freddy studied the china drawer pull on his bed table. "I'll have to be certain," he said.

"You will be," replied Pudding.

At that moment, Aunt Clara's green caterpillar slippers came slish-thudding down the hall. Freddy leaped up from the bed and swung the cage up with him.

"What are you going to do?" Pudding cried.

"Hide you in here," Freddy said, opening the door to his closet. He set the cage on the floor and threw over it a lavender plush frog, a baseball mit, and three beanbags. "Don't squeal or say a word!" he whispered to Pudding.

Pudding was half frozen with terror. "What will happen if Aunt Clara finds me?"

"Oh, she'll have Uncle Harry drown you in a bucket

of water," Freddy said blithely. "But don't worry about it!"

He slammed the closet door and thumped out of the room.

Pudding sat trembling in the darkness with Old Toaster's words ringing in his ears. "To them it's the sport that matters . . . seeing how long they can keep things alive in boxes and cages!"

THIRTEEN

Pop! Pop! Pop!

"Here, I've brought you something to eat," Freddy said. He slid the cage door up a crack and slipped under it a soggy little lump. Then he quickly dropped the door with a solid click. "I stole it from my breakfast," he said proudly.

Inside a small piece of damp paper napkin, Pudding found a teaspoonful of oatmeal and a ragged bit of limp toast. It was not very appetizing, but he tried to look pleased.

Freddy thumped down on the bed beside the cage. "Now, I want to hear everything. From the very beginning!"

The beginning seemed a long way back to Pudding, but there wasn't much he could do about it. He choked down the oatmeal and toast, made himself as comfortable as he could in a corner of the cage, and began, as Freddy had asked, "from the very beginning."

Pudding found it hard to remember everything he had learned about the Ages of the Elves, the Evil Ones, and the Heroes. Noah had taught him so very much. So at the beginning he got all the Ages mixed up, and forgot which Elf Hero slew which Elf Enemy. But the more he talked, the more he remembered. And as the days went by, the more he remembered, the more he talked.

"Wowee! Wowee!" Freddy exclaimed when an Elf battle was won by the Heroes, or an Elf Enemy lay writhing in mortal agony on the ground. He really was a very satisfying audience, Pudding found, and it was exciting to have Freddy's eager eyes on him as he spoke.

Freddy was kind to him, too. He always kept the water bowl in the cage filled. And when he discovered that Pudding didn't like the soggy little lumps he brought from the table, he began bringing sunflower seeds, berries, and rose hips from the garden. Sometimes they sucked sourgrass stalks together.

Pudding began to feel that things wouldn't be so bad if only he weren't looking out through the bars of a cage, or if he didn't have Old Toaster and Muddle to worry about. They would be terrified, not knowing where he was, or even if he were alive. He didn't dare send a message by Freddy. What if Freddy tried to capture *them*, too?

Pudding's only hope was to go on with the history and prove to Freddy that he really was an Elf. But at the end of every day's telling, Freddy would always reply, "I'm still not certain!"

More days passed by. At last, Pudding came to the part of the history where Furkens separated from the other Elves.

"Why did they?" Freddy asked.

"Nobody knows," Pudding told him. "They were the strongest, the bravest, the wildest, and the fiercest Elves of all, Noah said. Remember, Flinting and Bold-lock were Furkens. Nobody knows why they didn't move on with the other Elves and went into the dark places of Human houses instead. That was when they stopped being proper Elves. They hid in the dark like mice. They never stole like mice, and they never smelled like mice, but they became frightened like mice. So after a long time, they began to look like mice. It was when they became so frightened that they forgot how to—"

"Vanish!" cried Freddy. He clapped his hands excitedly.

"Yes!" Pudding said, and looked at Freddy with pleading eyes. "Don't you believe now that there really are Elves, and that's what I am?"

Freddy wiggled on the bed uncomfortably. Then he jumped up and walked to the window. He stood staring out for a long time. "I'm still not certain!" he said finally. He turned and blurted out, "I'm hungry. I think I'll go get something to eat." Then he clumped out of the room, leaving Pudding's cage sitting on his bed.

Pudding hurled himself down beside his sword. Tears rolled down his cheeks. He was certain now that Freddy would never let him go. He would be a prisoner forever, a descendant of the brave Elves, sitting out his life in a mouse cage! If he ever needed bravery, it was at this moment, when he suddenly felt as frightened as he'd ever felt in his life. But he knew now, finally and forever, that his sword couldn't give it to him. Nothing could!

Minutes passed, and still Freddy didn't return. But all at once another familiar sound came moving down the hall. It was the slish-thud, slish-thud of the green caterpillar slippers.

"Freddy! You'll have to get ready. We're going out in a short while. Freddy, where are you?" Aunt Clara's voice rang down the hall.

Pudding lay trembling on the floor of the cage. Already he could feel the water from the bucket rushing over him.

The slish-thud of the slippers entered the room, and there was a sudden, sharp shriek. "A mouse! Freddy! Freddy, come here this instant!" Aunt Clara screamed. "What is a mouse doing on your bed?" she cried hysterically as Freddy came pounding into the room.

Trapped in the cage, Pudding knew of only one thing he could do. It was something he hadn't tried in a very long time, and it had never worked before. Never-

theless, he closed his eyes tightly, held his breath until his
cheeks puffed out, and wished as hard as he could that he
wasn't a Furken. But nothing happened. He remained
solid as ever, quivering with fright behind the bars of the
cage.

"Dirty, stinking, nasty creature!" Aunt Clara
shrieked, seeming to have lost all control of herself at the
sight of this horror. "Where did you ever get him, Freddy? Did you find him in this house? You were lying to me,
weren't you, when you said you'd never seen a mouse?
Oh, I had a feeling we should never have moved into this
house. That crazy old man babbling about Elves. Freddy,
go telephone your Uncle Harry at work this instant. I
think I'm going to faint!"

As Aunt Clara screamed, Pudding clutched the hilt
of his sword. He held it at just the place where the three
little diamonds were set in. They dug into his hand so
hard that they hurt, the diamonds that stood for remembering, wanting, and believing.

Suddenly, as Aunt Clara hurled her terrible insults
at Pudding, a descendant of the strongest, bravest, wildest, and fiercest of all the Elves, there began to flash
through his mind, like pictures pulled on a string, all
the stories of Elf history he'd been telling Freddy. Each
picture was in his mind for only the smallest part of a
second, and yet it was clear and bright as if he had looked
at it for an hour in the sunlight. And when these pictures
had finished, new pictures began.

There was the picture of Old Toaster leaving his

home to come to a faraway, strange land. Wasn't that bravery? There was the picture of Old Toaster saying that he would wait in the house, by himself if he had to, for his friend Noah. Wasn't that courage? And finally, there was the picture of helpless Muddle setting out with a young boy, Pudding, to find a new home. Even if he made a mess of things and often made excuses, didn't it take a certain kind of courage to have tried at all? And wasn't it harder, after all, to be brave when you were quivering with fear inside than if you were just brave to start with?

Yes, Pudding told himself, he was proud of Old Toaster and Muddle and of all the Furkens. And he was proud to be a Furken, just as they were. If he had to die now, he would die bravely, as bravely as any Elf of old!

With this last thought, Pudding felt something curious happening to him. His head suddenly began to feel very, very light. It was a kind of drifty feeling, as if he was a dandelion seed being puffed by the wind. Then the rest of him began to feel steamy and wavy, the way air looks over moist earth when the sun reaches it. He felt as if he was swimming. No, it was more like floating through a sea of mist flavored with the nectar of honeysuckle, the fragrance of rose petals, and the swift clean scent of pine needles after the rain. It was clear as morning dew. It was something and nothing at the same time. It was an indescribable feeling of joy and wonder.

"Oh," Aunt Clara continued, moaning, "I don't think I can stand this. Oh, you filthy, horrible, nasty . . ."

Her voice faded, then stopped altogether. "Why, it's gone! There's nothing there. It's . . . it's *vanished*!"

Freddy's eyes flew open. "No, there isn't anything there. There . . ."—he hesitated—"there never was!"

"What do you mean? Are you trying to tell your Aunt Clara that she's seeing things? The mouse has escaped, that's what's happened. It's running around the room this instant!" Shrieking, she scrambled onto Freddy's bed.

"A mouse couldn't escape from that cage, Aunt Clara," Freddy said. "The bars are too close together, and the gate is locked. There really wasn't a mouse there. You . . . you just thought you saw one."

Aunt Clara's face turned a bright, embarrassed pink. She climbed quickly back down from the bed. "Well, no wonder, seeing a mouse cage sitting around like that. I want you to get rid of it at once!" She started out the door, weaving a little dizzily. "I'm certain I saw a mouse in that cage," she said in a weak voice. "I'm going to lie down awhile. Then I may call Dr. Folkes. I really haven't been feeling well lately."

Freddy looked down the hall to make certain his Aunt Clara had retreated to her room, then shut his door quietly. He went to his bed and picked up the cage. He shook it and turned it upside down and sideways. Then he set the cage back down on the bed, fell on his face beside it, and burst into tears.

"I believed all along that you were an Elf, Pudding.

I just didn't want anyone to think I was loony. But mostly I was afraid you'd run away if I let you out of the cage. I didn't want to lose you!" he sobbed.

"I haven't gone, Freddy!"

Freddy looked up in surprise. Pudding was standing by his hand. "I'm still here," he said.

"Pudding!" Freddy cried. "You're back! I thought you'd gone away forever. I . . . I wouldn't blame you if you had."

"I told you I wouldn't run away," Pudding said. "You had the word of an Elf. Elves don't lie."

"I do sometimes," said Freddy. Then all at once he sat up. He seemed to have forgotten that he'd just been crying. His eyes were shining. "How did you vanish, Pudding? Can you do it again?"

Pudding promptly vanished and then reappeared a moment later, smiling broadly. "It's simple. You just have to be proud you're a Furken instead of wishing you weren't one!"

"But how do you un-vanish?" Freddy asked.

"That's simple, too," Pudding replied. "You just wish yourself back again." To Freddy's clear delight, he vanished and reappeared quickly three times in a row. Pop! Pop! Pop! Like a flash bulb.

"I wish I could vanish!" Freddy said eagerly. "I smell good. At least after my bath, I do. I don't steal. I haven't since I was six, anyway. I'm proud of myself, too." He stopped to think this over a moment. "Sometimes," he added. "Do you suppose I could vanish?"

"Those are all nice things," Pudding said, "but you're not an Elf, Freddy. So I guess you'll never be able to vanish. Not the way I do, anyway. But believing in Elves is the next best thing. And now you do that!"

"Yes, I do!" said Freddy earnestly. "But what are you going to do now, Pudding? Will you stay with me? I'll fix up the barrel in the basement just the way it was before. You can live there. Aunt Clara never goes near it. She says it gives her the creeps. You'll be safe. Oh, I forgot!" Freddy laughed. "It doesn't matter now. You can vanish!"

"I'd like to live in the barrel again," Pudding said. "But there's a journey I must make first. You'll have to help me with it."

Freddy looked surprised. "What can *I* do to help *you*?"

"You'll have to find out about Noah and Thor from your Aunt Clara and Uncle Harry. I'm going to rescue them, and I have to find out where they are."

"I'd like to help," Freddy said, "really I would. But I can't ask Aunt Clara and Uncle Harry something like that. They'd be suspicious in a minute. Isn't there anyone else who might know?"

Pudding thought hard for a moment. "There isn't anyone who knows, but there's someone who might be able to find out."

"Who?"

"A cat named Marvin lives across the street. Cats have friends everywhere. I'll ask him if he can find out anything."

"Is Marvin your friend?" Freddy asked.

"Not exactly," Pudding replied. "But he can't hurt me now. I'll go see him."

"Please, oh please, let me go with you!" Freddy pleaded.

"I don't see why you shouldn't," Pudding said. "You can take me in your pocket."

"Wowee!" said Freddy, scooping Pudding up in his hands. "I've always wanted to carry something small and soft and furry in my shirt pocket!"

"That's what I thought!" Pudding said.

They found Marvin sunning himself in the empty lot across the street. He looked a lot thinner than the last time Pudding had seen him. He was dozing peacefully by an empty mayonnaise jar.

"Sit down near him," Pudding whispered to Freddy, "then put me in your hand."

"Psssst, Marvin!" Pudding hissed. "It's me, the what-kin!"

Marvin's eyes barely opened into two pale green slits. When he saw Pudding sitting on Freddy's hand, he shuddered and groaned. "Go away! I don't want to get mixed up with you again. You were the cause of a long and serious illness. I don't care if you're a whatkin or what you are. Just go away and leave me alone!"

"All right, I'll go away," said Pudding. Pop! He disappeared from Freddy's hand.

Freddy giggled. "That tickles!"

Pudding appeared again.

"Don't do that!" Marvin groaned. "All right, so you're an Elf. You've made your point. Now what is it you want. Please tell me and then go away."

"I want you to help me find out where Noah and Thor are," Pudding said.

"Why?" Marvin asked suspiciously.

"I'm going to rescue them."

"You?" Marvin sneered. "What can anyone your size do?"

"This!" said Pudding, and disappeared again.

"All right, all right!" snapped Marvin.

Pudding reappeared.

"Well"—Marvin looked nervously around the lot—"it so happens I've already found out where they are."

"What did he say?" Freddy asked Pudding excitedly.

"He says he already knows where they are!"

"Wowee!" exclaimed Freddy. "How did he do that?"

"My friend, Freddy, wants to know how you did it," said Pudding.

"Actually it's none of his business," Marvin said rudely. Still, he looked a little pleased with himself.

"But you can tell him I've got connections."

"He's got connections," repeated Pudding. "It's just as I said."

"Wowee!" said Freddy.

"Will you tell me where Noah and Thor are then, please?" Pudding asked.

Marvin groaned. "Well, if I must, I must. Ask your friend if he can draw a map."

Pudding relayed the question to Freddy, and Freddy proudly pulled a grubby pencil stub from his second pocket.

"What's he going to write on?" Marvin snorted.

Pudding repeated the question to Freddy.

"I can go back for paper," Freddy said eagerly. "No, wait, here's an empty soup tin. I can draw a map on the wrapper."

Marvin flicked his tail and sighed.

Fifteen minutes later, with Pudding relaying the instructions from Marvin, Freddy had drawn the map. It was scrawled all around the tin. Two x's on the map showed where Noah and Thor were being held prisoner.

Pudding studied it carefully. "Thank you, Marvin!"

"Never mind the frills," Marvin replied ungraciously. "Just tell your friend to put you back in his pocket, take his soup tin, and then all of you please leave!" He closed his eyes wearily.

As Pudding and Freddy left the lot, he called after them in a weak voice, "Tell Thor I send my regards." Then he collapsed in the sun like a fur rag.

"Well, now you know where Noah and Thor are, but how will you rescue them, Pudding? What will you do?" Freddy asked as soon as they had returned to his room.

Pudding slid his sword into its sheath. "Rescuing Thor will be easy. All I have to do is find the key to his cage and unlock it. Noah might be a bit more difficult. You see, Thor told me Noah's cousins were waiting for the chance to tuck him away." Pudding scowled. "I guess they got their chance all right, when he became sick. I suspect he became downhearted as well and forgot all about the stars of remembering, wanting and believing. Most likely he's even been persuaded that he really is loony."

"But when you show up, he won't think it anymore, will he?" Freddy asked.

"That's exactly what I'm hoping," replied Pudding. "Then when he learns that even a Furken can get back his bravery . . . *well*! He'll be equal to anything!"

"Oh Pudding, that sounds terrific!" Freddy said. "But once the cousins find Noah's gone, won't they come after him and try to tuck him away again?"

"Ha!" exploded Pudding, unsheathing his sword and slashing it fiercely through the air. "Just let them try!"

"Wowee!" shouted Freddy. He began to dance around his room until all at once another thought came to him and he stopped, his face solemn. "What . . . what if you decide never to come back here?"

"Oh, I'll be back. I have to come back."

"But what if you don't," Freddy insisted. "There's nothing here for you to come back to except me."

"That's enough, Freddy! But it so happens there *is* more than just you. Behind . . ." Pudding hesitated. ". . . behind the crack in the ceiling where I came from are Old Toaster and Muddle. They're two more Elves just like me!"

Freddy's eyes popped. "Two more! Why didn't you ever tell me before? Oh, I know why. You didn't trust me, did you?"

"That's right!" said Pudding.

"Do you trust me now, *really* trust me?"

Pudding gave a firm nod.

Freddy grinned happily. "I won't try to capture them, I promise. I'll watch over them, but I won't bother them. Tell them they'll be perfectly safe until you come for them. But . . . but then where will you go? You love this house, and we're living in it."

"The house isn't important," Pudding said. "What's important is that we're together, wherever we are."

Freddy stared at the floor for a long time. When he looked up again at Pudding, his lashes were wet with tears. "But 'together' is you and Old Toaster and Muddle and Noah and Thor. 'Together' doesn't have 'me' in it."

"Maybe not now," said Pudding. "But just remember, if I can go get Noah and Thor . . . I can always go get you, can't I?"

FOURTEEN

It's Me!

"Wh . . . wh . . . wh . . . who's there?" gasped Muddle.

Pudding giggled. "It's me . . . Pudding!"

"It's no such thing!" warned Old Toaster. "It's a trick, or a trap. Don't move, Muddle!"

"But I heard Pudding's voice, I tell you," Muddle insisted. "I ought to know it. I've taken care of him since I found him under the walnut shell. Shouldn't I know his voice when I hear it?"

"Not when you're befuddled by all that's happened. We both are, Muddle. We don't know what we're hearing or seeing anymore."

"But it really is me, Old Toaster," Pudding said. "Muddle's right. I've vanished . . . and come back!"

"Y . . . y . . . y . . . you're not a g . . . g . . . g . . . ghost, are you?" Muddle was pale as one himself.

"Here," said Pudding, "does this feel like a ghost?" He dug Muddle in the ribs, and suddenly appeared, smiling, before his friend

"Pudding! Pudding, it's you!" Muddle threw his arms around Pudding in a fierce hug. Tears coursed down his round cheeks.

When Muddle finally let him go, Old Toaster coughed politely and held out his hand to Pudding. Pudding put his own hand out and then, suddenly, to his surprise, found Old Toaster's bony arms around him. The old Furken's cheeks, pressed against his, were wet. Then he just as suddenly withdrew his arms and, pretending busily to be adjusting his muffler, secretly wiped his eyes on the fringe.

"Vanished!" Muddle said. "Did you say *'vanished'*?"

"Vanished!" Pudding repeated merrily, and promptly disappeared from Muddle's and Old Toaster's sight.

"Well, by the great horn-tailed dragon. Vanished! Did you see that, Toaster?" Muddle said proudly.

"I did indeed!" replied Old Toaster.

Pudding popped back into sight.

"How did you manage it? Pudding, tell us!" Muddle pleaded.

"Well, it's a very long story and starts way back from the day I was captured in Freddy's cage."

"Captured by the boy! I said as much!" exclaimed Old Toaster.

"W . . . w . . . w . . . we thought you were dead!" said Muddle, his eyes filling with tears again.

"I was afraid you might," said Pudding, "but there wasn't anything I could do about it. At the beginning I was afraid Freddy might capture you, too! At any rate, this is how it all happened."

And Pudding told them his story.

"You're certain the boy said he wouldn't come near us?" Old Toaster's voice was trembling.

"I'm certain!" said Pudding firmly. "I told him he could meet you when I get back. You'll like him. I know you will!"

A wistful, faraway look crept into Muddle's eyes. "Vanish! Do you suppose Old Toaster and I could ever vanish?"

"I'm much too old," Old Toaster said, shaking his head sadly. He did look old, too, like a shriveled up old carpetbag.

"You said you were too old to dance again, but you did!" Pudding told him. "I believe you could both vanish. I believe any Furken could. I'm not quite sure myself yet how it happens, but I believe it has to do with what Noah said, remembering things past, wanting, and believing, and . . . and being proud of yourself."

"P . . . p . . . p . . . proud? Of *me?*" Muddle's face seemed torn between wondering whether it should look pleased, or simply astonished at this remarkable thought.

"You've got lots to be proud of, Muddle," Pudding said. "Being frightened doesn't always mean not being brave. Think how you brought us to our new home! And think how Old Toaster left his old home to come to a strange land with Noah. And how you both decided to wait here for him even with danger in the house. Think about the Furkens of old, and how you're one of them. Think about it *very hard*, and you'll be able to vanish one day. I'm certain of it!"

"Certain?" said Muddle in a faraway voice.

"Certain!" said Pudding. "And now I have to leave. You'll be safe here. Freddy will see that you are."

"Do . . . do you think you'll really be able to rescue Noah and Thor?" Muddle asked.

Pudding laughed aloud. "Of course I will! Muddle, I can *vanish* now! A Furken who can vanish can do anything in the whole world he wants to. He can battle with rats. He can live in a barrel in a basement or . . ." He dug Muddle mischievously in the ribs. ". . . or in a tree trunk. And he can rescue *anyone*! Don't worry!" Pudding threw his arms around Muddle and hugged him. "I'll be back with Noah and Thor before you can say 'vanish'!"

He turned and, ignoring Old Toaster's outstretched hand, gave him a hug equal to the one he had given Muddle. Then, before the look of surprise and pleasure had left the old Furken's face, Pudding was running down the ledge toward the tunnel.

A moment later, he stepped through the little door with the mushroom handle out into the garden. An early clump of firethorn berries burned bright red in the bushes behind him. The sunlight lay in quiet patches on the moss, glistening off a tiny yellow bird's feather that lay captured in a soft green mossy fold. Pudding picked up the feather and tucked it jauntily behind one ear. Then he looked up at the house. A nose, with two bright blue eyes over it, was pressed tightly against an upstairs window. Pudding waved, and a hand waved back.

He grasped the hilt of his sword firmly and drew in his breath. Pop! A tiny blade of grass quivered as if a puff of wind had blown over it. It was the only reminder left in the garden that a Furken had been there—and vanished.